# A GUIDE TO ANIMAL BEHAVIOUR

**Books by Douglas Glover**

*The Mad River*
*Precious*
*Dog Attempts to Drown Man in Saskatoon*
*The South Will Rise at Noon*

# A GUIDE TO ANIMAL BEHAVIOUR

## DOUGLAS GLOVER

GOOSE LANE

Published with the assistance of the Canada Council, 1991.

The author would like to thank the Canada Council and the Ontario Arts Council for their support while this book was being written.

*A Guide to Animal Behaviour* is a work of fiction. All the characters herein are imaginary and any resemblance to actual people, living or dead, is strictly coincidental.

Cover painting: "Alterpiece # 1" (detail) by Lindee Climo, 1989, oil on canvas, 117 cm x 168 cm, courtesy Nancy Poole's Studio.
Back cover photo by Sylvia Oostijen-Matsumura.
Book design by Julie Scriver.
Printed in Canada by Ronalds Printing.

Canadian Cataloguing in Publication Data

Glover, Douglas, 1948-
   A guide to animal behaviour

ISBN 0-86492-136-5

I. Title.

PS8563.L68G84 1991   C813'.54   C91-097555-8
PR9199.3.G56G84 1991

Goose Lane Editions
248 Brunswick Street
Fredericton, New Brunswick
Canada E3B 1G9

# ACKNOWLEDGEMENTS

Some of these stories have been previously published in the following magazines and anthologies.

"Story Carved in Stone" in *Descant*, Vol. 19, No. 3, Fall 1988; *The Journey Prize Anthology* (Toronto: McClelland and Stewart, 1990). "Story Carved in Stone" won the 1990 National Magazine Award for Fiction.

"Swain Corliss, Hero of Malcolm's Mills (now Oakland, Ontario), November 6, 1814" in *The Quarterly*, No. 13, Spring 1990.

"Why I Decide to Kill Myself and Other Jokes" in *The Fiddlehead*, No. 155, Spring 1988; *The Journal of Literary Translation*, Vol. 20, Spring 1988; *88 Best Canadian Stories* (Ottawa: Oberon Press, 1988); *Best American Short Stories* (Boston: Houghton-Mifflin, 1989).

"The Canadian Travel Notes of Abbé Hugues Pommier, Painter, 1663-1680" in *Fire Beneath The Cauldron* (Saskatoon: Thistledown Press, 1990).

"The Obituary Writer" in *87 Best Canadian Stories* ( Ottawa: Oberon Press, 1987); *Canadian Fiction Magazine*, No. 65, 1989.

"Turned into a Horse by Witches, Port Rowan, U.C., 1798" in *This Magazine*, Vol. 21, No. 2, May-June 1987; *Open Win-*

*dows: Canadian Short-short Stories* (Kingston: Quarry Press, 1988).

"A Guide to Animal Behaviour" in *The Iowa Review,* Vol. 17, No. 2, Spring-Summer 1987; *Open Windows: Canadian Short-short Stories* (Kingston: Quarry Press, 1988).

"I, A Young Man Called Early to the Wars" in *The Fiddlehead,* No. 144, Summer 1985.

"The Travesty of Sleep" in *Canadian Fiction Magazine,* No. 67/68, 1989; *The Third Macmillan Anthology* (Toronto: Macmillan, 1990).

"Woman Gored by Bison Lives" in *The Third Macmillan Anthology* (Toronto: Macmillan, 1990).

For Helen

# CONTENTS

# STORY CARVED IN STONE

I thought my wife had left me, but she is back. What she has been doing the last two years, I have no idea. She's thinner. She has a Princess Di haircut, and she's wearing tight, three-quarter-length, white sweatpants and a black blouse. She's sitting across from me at the kitchen table, looking self-possessed and aloof. Her name is Glenna. She won't speak to me.

I make her a cup of instant coffee which she ignores. I do not press her with idle questions because, to tell the truth, she terrifies me. Brent Wardlow down the street had his wife leave five years ago. When she came back six months later, driving a new Eldorado with fluffy dice dangling from the rearview mirror, Brent asked her one question, and she was gone again the next day. Sitting down at the Dunkin' Donut on a weekday morning, he allows that he has learned his lesson and will keep his mouth shut the next time she returns.

I am not saying that my situation is exactly the same as Brent's — everyone in Ragged Point knows he drove his wife out with excessive golf playing and sexual demands — but a word to the wise, etc. Also, I have checked the driveway, and it is evident that Glenna did not drive home in an Eldorado. Everything she has is packed in a brown United Airlines shoulder-bag, with the zipper popped, and a small, black pocketbook decorated with spangles.

We sit for a couple of hours like this, not talking, Glenna just staring at the kitchen window where the lace half-curtains she made are turning somewhat dingy for lack of a woman's care. As she watches, the window fills with purple sunset, then blackens like a bruise. The only sound comes from the bug-zapper in the breezeway, killing insects. At 9 p.m., Glenna heaves a sigh, whether of relief at being home again or of sadness, I cannot tell. Then she gathers her shoulder-bag and pocketbook into her arms and walks down the hall to the guest bedroom.

I hear the guest bedroom door lock. I hear water running in the bathroom. Presently, I am disturbed by the sound of sobs, the sound of Glenna weeping with wild abandon. I am torn as to whether or not I should run to comfort her. But I recall Brent Wardlow's experience and decide to leave well enough alone.

Instead of knocking on the guest bedroom door, I head outside into the darkness. Turning past the bug-zapper and the lurid pink neon GULF HAVEN, VACANCY sign, past the nine identical one-room holiday housekeeping cottages, painted coral, with red trim and matching concrete parking pads, past the peach tree just coming into blossom, the oyster cookery and the little dock where I keep my John boat, I stop at the tenth cottage, which is not identical — forest-green with weathered trim, cracked panes in the windows and a porch roof buttressed with two-by-fours.

"Mama," I say, bursting in, "Glenna's back!"

To tell the truth, I am pretty excited. Nothing this big has happened since Glenna left, and before that, not since my father died in a boating accident (he was leaning out of the boat to retrieve his oyster fork, fell overboard and suffered a heart attack — his last words to me were, "Shit, E.A., the fork's stuck!").

Mama's cottage is dark as a cave. She sits at a deal table, the glow of her cigarette lighting up her face, a frozen orange juice can full of butts on one hand, a glass and a pile of wrung-out lime slices on the other. She takes an extra long drag on her cigarette, then breaks into a coughing spasm.

"The whore," she says, finally, and I rush out again.

For an hour I stand watching the bug-zapper, its eerie blue glow and the flashes and sparks it gives off as it does its work. A young couple in Cabin Six is making noisy and acrobatic love; the Firbanks, old regulars who have been coming here since my father built the place just after the war, are listening through their open window. My wife's sobbing has subsided, though I am convinced she is not asleep, only staring at the ceiling, listening to the bugs dying and the distant love sounds.

In the morning, I rise early and drive to Biloxi for supplies: croissants, real coffee, fresh butter, Glenna's favourite marmalade, a New Orleans TIMES-PICAYUNE and white napkins. While I am making breakfast, I hear her stirring at the other end of the house. I hear the shower running, then I hear her soft voice singing. I can't make out the words, but I know it's a hymn.

I am sugaring my coffee, listening to Glenna, when Mrs. Firbank knocks at the back door. She has come to complain about the young couple in Cabin Six.

If there is anything the Firbanks cannot stand, it is young people having fun on their vacation (to think that when I was a boy I used to call them Uncle Ted and Aunt Netty). During the Firbanks' annual two-week stay, Cabin Eight becomes a veritable black hole of joy, and I am under constant pressure to turn Gulf Haven into a police state.

Needless to say, they are great friends of Mama's, and there is much toing and froing between their respective lairs, where they drink and reflect together on the bitter emptiness of life. Though my father willed Gulf Haven to me, all three of them regard me as a form of renter, a temporary interloper with no idea how to run a successful business.

Mrs. Firbank believes something "funny" was going on in Cabin Six last night. She has noted a "peculiar odour" and heard "nigger music" played on the radio. Above all, she wishes me to demand to see the young couple's marriage licence.

"Maybe I'd better get Sheriff Buck to run their plate number through the computer," I suggest, having learned never to argue a moral point with a guest.

When I finally shut the door on Mrs. Firbank's righteous back, I turn to find Glenna sitting at the table, a knowing smile on her lips. She's wearing the white sweatpants and black blouse, but her pink feet are bare, and her hair is swathed in a towel turban.

For Glenna, the most difficult thing about life at Gulf Haven was dealing with the public, especially with guests like the Firbanks. She much preferred helping Effie, our black chambermaid, with the cleaning, and made a show of mocking my secretive politeness. Mealy-mouthed is what she called it. Though, when she said the words, she would laugh and roll her eyes as if to say, "I know what you're up to, you."

To see her smiling now in our kitchen feels like a gift from God, and I turn quickly to hide the mist that comes to my eyes. It is like old times, except that I dare not say a word (remembering what happened to Brent) and Glenna will not speak to me. I am almost paralysed with fear and hope. I know she is capable of leaving again the minute my back is turned, the first mistake I make.

Out the window, I see Mama conversing with the Firbanks next to their vintage Dodge Satellite. They keep looking in our direction, and I know Mama is telling them the good news about Glenna. Mama has a glass and a cigarette in one hand and a claw-hammer in the other. The claw-hammer is a constant, silent rebuke to me. She is always "repairing" something on the property and holding up the sorry state of her own cottage as evidence that she doesn't have a moment to spare to look after herself.

The truth is that Effie's husband, Bubba, and I keep the place up with very little effort. We are always trying to fix Mama's cottage, but she throws a fit every time we go near it. She says Bubba "watches" her. It took us three years to remove a limb that fell on her roof during Hurricane Camille.

When I turn back to Glenna with the tray of croissants and marmalade, her face has gone cold again. She sips her coffee but refuses to eat the meal I have made for her. I bite my tongue to keep from saying, "A person can't live on coffee alone." If anything, she is more ravishing now than when she left, her body a geometry of angles and curves like one of those magazine models.

Then my watch alarm sounds, telling me it is time to go outside and supervise the help. In fact there is little supervision to be done. Only I must be on hand to prevent Effie from barging in on the young couple in Cabin Six. Effie is a large, lusty woman who delights in breaking in on guests, especially when they are in the throes of passion, sometimes scaring them half to death with her booming laughter. She is a great displayer of used condoms and is always on the lookout for signs of perverse practices.

As I stand to leave, I allow myself a quick glance at my wife, who is staring at the wall. Her expression is a sermon of loss, and it is with great difficulty that I restrain myself from throwing my arms around her. But I am prevented by the thought that I do not know where she's been or what she wants or what she has lost. With Glenna now, anything is possible.


At 11 a.m., I am sitting on a stool at the Dunkin' Donut, Bubba on my right, Brent Wardlow on my left. The place is crowded with fishermen, shopkeepers, resort owners, hardware salesmen and local clergy, all shouting, laughing and gesticulating. Everyone knows that Glenna is back, and I am the centre of attention. The booths and counter stools are alive with noisy speculation on motives, itineraries and outcomes. Each new topic is quickly exhausted for lack of hard facts. Questions break out and spread across the room like grass fires, and I am continually saying, "I just don't know."

Everyone understands why I hesitate to ask Glenna direct questions. Besides Brent, many men in Ragged Point have lost wives, permanently or temporarily. Intuitively, we all recognize that this is an age of adventure for women. We are learning to respect their privacy, just as they are learning the special pain of being free and responsible people. It is not easy; it is like watching some great and beautiful creature being born.

The facts are these: two years ago, Glenna slipped out of the house at dawn and walked over to Moody's Fish Restaurant to catch the morning Greyhound for Biloxi. She wore a cotton print dress with a white belt and carried, according to Darrell Moody who sold her the ticket, an alligator-skin purse I had given her for Christmas and a Land's End canvas briefcase we shared for business purposes. She had seemed, Darrell recalls now, especially cheerful, and, with her coral lipstick and faint trail of eyeliner, "so pretty she hurt your eyes."

She headed inland from Biloxi. Sheriff Buck and I interrogated a ticket agent who swore she had paid for as far as Nashville. Lois Motherwell, Andy Motherwell's mother and a Grand Ole Opry fan, claimed to have spotted her at a Merle Haggard concert that night, though Sheriff Buck discounted her story on the grounds that she did not think of it till three months later.

In Nashville, we lost Glenna's trail. We know she didn't linger because the sheriff turned that city upside-down searching for her. But, except for a state trooper who thought he recalled "a lady with a briefcase hitchhiking north," we had no other clue.

By 11:30, we have reached a consensus plan of action. I am to use my insider position to add whatever snippets I can to our precious store of information, using my eyes and ears but not my mouth. "Like a fly on the wall," someone says. I forget who.

Bubba swears he will tell me anything Effie lets drop, though we agree he must not appear to "pump" her. Brent Wardlow suggests checking her clothing for store tags or dry cleaning stubs. Sand caught in the seams might indicate she has been to the seashore. Sheriff Buck advises getting a look at that United Airlines bag for transit tags.

Above all, I must not arouse suspicion. Everyone agrees that Glenna must be the first to speak. I must not appear upset or condescending. Brent says I ought to act "as normal as possible."

As Bubba and I stroll along the breakwater toward Gulf Haven, I feel a sudden rush of belonging, of brotherhood. My pessimism evaporates, my spirits begin to rise. I grasp Bubba by the shoulder and make him stop. When he looks into my face, he understands.

"Sure 'nough," he says, clapping his pink palms with glee. "Sure 'nough," he hoots.

He takes my hand and leads me a step or two in a little

tango dance. The noon sun catches us there, freezes us in its opaque whiteness, two men dancing under the cabbage palms.

She's back.


At Gulf Haven, a scene awaits us that brings my heart to my mouth.

The Firbanks' Satellite is parked across the gravel drive next to the neon sign, forming a roadblock. Someone has tried to squeeze my utility van past the Satellite, only to get it stuck in the azaleas. The driver's door gapes open, the engine is running. A Datsun station wagon belonging to the young couple in Cabin Six has nosed up to the Satellite, and the young couple is standing next to it, waiting to drive out. The Firbanks hover at the bottom step of the stone porch, watching Mama and Effie grapple together at the door. Mama has a death grip on the handle latch. Effie is trying to peel her fingers off.

"You leave her alone, Mizz Toby," says Effie, as Bubba and I run up. "You leave Glenna alone."

"Let go of my hand," gasps Mama, who has bad lungs and is turning blue from the exercise. Seeing me, she suddenly abandons the struggle.

"Never mind," she says, her eyes savage with triumph. "E.A.'s here. E.A., she's locked us out. She tried to leave in your van, but Ted Firbank foxed her."

Glenna is not in sight, though I am certain she can hear every word I say.

"I believe it's *our* van, Mama," I begin. "Just as much hers as mine."

"E.A. Toby, you can't be serious. She was going to steal it and run off again."

I do not know why Mama hates Glenna so much (maybe it is only that my wife is still young and has all her hopes before her) or why she is so down on life. But there have been times in the past when I have considered murdering her for the benefit of mankind. And now it takes all my powers of self-restraint to keep from committing a crime against a person I love for which the state gives lethal injections.

"Ted," I say, nodding toward the Satellite, "you think you could move your car? I appreciate the help and all, but the other guests will want to get out."

Then I race around by the rock path to the back door, hurrying inside before Mama catches her breath and follows me.

A shadow slips down the hall into the guest bedroom. The house is silent except that I am almost sure I can hear Glenna's heart beating. Then I notice a slip of paper and a pencil stub on the kitchen table. Trembling, I begin to read.

"E.A., I wasn't stealing the van. I just wanted — "

The letters slope off drunkenly and stop, as though she lost heart with her explanation, as though she realized how futile and humiliating it was to make any explanation at all. But it is still a note, a message addressed to me. It is something. I suddenly forget myself and stride down the hall. I pause at the guest bedroom door and listen. She is crying again, but muffling it. I can barely stand the pain she is in.

I take a ballpoint from the plastic penholder in my breast pocket and scribble beneath her words: "G., You don't have to tell me." I add the phrase, "Welcome home," but black it out. Then, "I love you," and black that out, too. The pen slips in my sweaty fingers and skips as I try to write against the door. I end the note with "Love, E.A." and leave it at that.

Then I knock softly and push through.

Glenna is sitting on the bed, hunched over, with the

United Airlines bag cradled in her arms. When I hand her the note, she straightens up, pushes her hair back defiantly and rubs the heel of her palm across her lip.

She stares at the piece of paper for five minutes. Maybe she is trying to decipher the blacked-out phrases. Maybe this is just an excuse not to look at me. Anyway, I know it doesn't take five minutes to read a six-word message.

I take advantage of these minutes, though, to look around the room. There are some female things on the counter in the bathroom, combs, hair dryer, Tampax, conditioners and shampoos. Beyond that, she doesn't seem to have unpacked anything. I peer at the airline bag, pondering its secrets. In fact, there are a couple of baggage tags, and I memorize the codes to give to Sheriff Buck.

Glenna begins to rummage in her pocketbook. I offer her a tissue from the box on the dresser, but she shakes her head no without looking at me. Then I hold out one of my pens, which she takes. She turns the note over and begins to write.

"E.A.," I read, standing next to her, then she stops to think.

Inadvertently, my hand brushes her shoulder. A wisp of hair trails across my knuckles. Nothing more. And it wasn't anything I meant to do, not a caress or a liberty I was taking. But she twists away.

She writes, "E.A., Don't touch me. Don't come in this room again. Don't expect anything from me."

I reel backward toward the door, wounded, sweaty and feeling like a fool. My eyes sting. But I glance back once before I leave, and she is staring at me. When she reaches up to press a tear from her cheek with a forefinger, I see the tan line where her wedding ring used to be. She sees that I see and, pressing the hand into her lap, covers it with the other.

The look in her eyes is neither angry nor apologetic.

Suddenly I see how she has changed. Though she trembles and tears spring to her eyes, she carries herself with a new and unaccountable dignity, as though she has learned some secret about sorrow and tragedy.

Later, in the office, after I have recovered and checked in two sets of new guests, I call Sheriff Buck with the transit codes. At first, he is boyishly excited, but then he catches the grave, neutral tone in my voice and senses that I have begun to stop caring about the rabbit hunt into Glenna's past. In ten minutes, he telephones back.

"Shit, E.A.," he says, "she went to the North Pole. She went clear up into Canada. Way up, E.A.! Those tickets are for flights between Montreal and some diddly little place with an Indian name. I can't even find it on the road atlas. There ain't nothing but ice and snow where Glenna's been."

I hang up, not wishing to hear more, and imagine my wife journeying north from the summer heat of Ragged Point, away from everything she'd ever known, north into another country, to where the people and houses begin to thin out, north beyond the tree-line, to a desert of ice and rock. I take out the NATIONAL GEOGRAPHIC ATLAS I keep in the office and look up the place Sheriff Buck has named. It is a dot on an otherwise empty island far above the Arctic Circle. Someone has drawn an X over it with red ink.


During the night, I am afflicted with nightmares. As soon as my head hits the pillow, I find myself in a world of twisting, heaving ice. Everywhere I turn, seams of gray water open up with a fearful ripping sound. In the distance, I make out a figure, drifting away from me. A great, white bear looms above her — I feel sure it means to take her in its ugly embrace and bite her head off.

I scream, "Glenna! Glenna!"

When I awake, I am crying into my pillow, and my wife stands in the doorway, her face set in an expression of stern and terrible pity. She says nothing, but continues to stare at me as though trying to puzzle something out. I am all twisted up in sheets sodden with sweat, and, for a time, I am uncertain whether this is still the dream or not.

Glenna wears pale blue baby-doll pajamas which I gave her on a birthday and which she must have retrieved from our dresser drawer earlier in the day. Poised in the moonlight, she is all legs and eyes. The odours of her shampoo and bath powder cause me pangs of nostalgia worse than any pain I have felt since she left.

I want to cry out again. I want to pretend I am still asleep so that under the guise of unconsciousness I might tell her of all my secret fears, my nights of loneliness, my mute love. But, presently, with Glenna standing there, I really do fall asleep. When I wake up again, solitary in our nuptial Posturpedic, it is to the sound of the van door slamming shut and the engine catching. The terrors of my dreams return. For a while, I cannot move, can only listen as the van sound disappears in the distance.

When I finally stumble into the breezeway in my boxer shorts, the morning sun is like a drop of blood on the horizon, and Mama is standing next to the Firbanks' banana-yellow Satellite with a cigarette and her claw-hammer and a look of silent judgment on her face.


The men at the Dunkin' Donut are quiet and constrained. It is clear from Brent Wardlow's stricken eyes that he believes Ragged Point has lost another wife for good.

Sheriff Buck tells how he staked out Gulf Haven for half the night, expecting Glenna to make a break for it after the way Mama treated her. He had intended to flag her down on the coast road and remonstrate with her. But something held him back.

"It just didn't feel right, E.A., trailing her in the dark. It peels my guts. But she's got her own life to live, you know what I mean? I'm sorry, bud."

I nod and sip my coffee, pretending that the moisture in my eyes is because my tongue is burned. Even at a distance, Sheriff Buck has sensed Glenna's new, inviolable dignity. I tell the men about the NATIONAL GEOGRAPHIC ATLAS and the tiny red x.

"There'd be Eskimos," says Elder Ottman, the Baptist minister, "maybe a mission or a government store, maybe even one of those Royal Canadian Mounties." Eyebrows shoot up. "Eskimos," he adds, "means 'eaters of raw meat.'"

"Gawd!" says Bubba, spluttering into a napkin.

An uncomfortable silence follows. I have not mentioned my nightmares or the vision of Glenna standing in the doorway. The men are too sensitive to press for intimate details. It is all so painful. Every word, every gesture, is understood to be a many-levelled message of commiseration, shared hopelessness and awe. For there is a restlessness amongst the women of Ragged Point, as there is amongst the women of the nation, as though they have all inhaled some passing interplanetary dust.

Elder Ottman's wife recently stopped watching soap operas and began to check books on oil painting out of the town library. Lois Motherwell, Andy's mother, has moved a typewriter into the boathouse, neglecting her duties in the drygoods store, and claims to be writing a novel. Five young mothers have hired a babysitter and spend their afternoons hang-gliding off Rattler Peak.

To tell the truth, when the husbands relate these exploits, mornings at the Dunkin' Donut, it is not difficult to detect a note of pride in their voices. As well as anxiety. For who knows (this is the common feeling, never expressed in so many words), who knows where it will end?

Our meditation is shattered suddenly by the arrival of Stu Bollis, the man who drives the fish-delivery truck. Horn blaring, he nearly dents Sheriff Buck's municipal Plymouth in his rush to park.

"She ain't gone, E.A.!" he exclaims, pushing the screen door open with a slap. "She ain't gone. I knew you'd think she was gone the minute I saw the van."

"Where is she, Stu?" I ask, trying to shake loose the skin of ice congealing over my thoughts.

"Down at the point, parked in the pines. I seen her sitting on the rocks, with her pants rolled up, just looking out at the water. I reckon she is thinking, don't you?"

I nod to Sheriff Buck, who grabs his Stetson as he and Bubba come after me. He lays rubber down Water Street, pops the siren once for the stoplight at Jefferson Davis, then hits sixty-five leaving town. At the Ragged Point turn-off, he pulls a U-turn and drops me on the gravel. He and Bubba give me the thumbs-up as they head out.

I walk nervously through the pines where the van is parked, past the log barrier, picnic tables and wire trash baskets and onto the rocks. Tide is out. Pelicans and laughing gulls cruise a hair's breadth above the waves. Glenna is seated just as Stu described her, only there is a pile of fresh sand dollars drying next to her hip and her feet are sandy and wet.

She looks up and smiles. We both glance toward town and see Sheriff Buck's Plymouth creeping along Water Street so that he and Bubba can keep us in sight as long as possible.

Glenna shakes her head and giggles, then lies back on her elbows and preens in the sun. Her expression says, "Oh my, I had forgotten how much I love the heat" — a sentiment I can surely understand, considering where she has been.

But her look also fills me with sadness for what I have lost. In spite of my resolve to keep things upbeat, I suddenly have to put my hand over my face to suppress a sob. It is only natural to want things to stay the way they are. I love the new Glenna, maybe more than the old. But she is different now, aloof and unapproachable.

Then I become aware of Glenna's hand touching mine on the tidal rock. It is an electric gesture that sends a thrill into my bones. She covers my hand with hers, then takes it up and laces her fingers between mine. I dare not look at her. I dare not say a word. I dare not even return pressure for pressure against her slim and fragile digits.

My wife stands and pulls me up. I keep my eyes steadily fixed on the gulf, with its comforting emptiness festering under the sun. All is vanity, the slapping waves tell me. All is flesh, and the flesh abideth not.

We collect the sand dollars in my baseball cap. Somewhere between the water and the van, she takes my hand again.


Gulf Haven is just as we have left it, except that the back door stands open, and our house has the atmosphere of a desolate cave. It is also unusual not to see the Firbanks sitting in their lawn chairs next to the Satellite, drinking from high-ball glasses and casting sour and disapproving glances at everything through their aviator Ray-Bans. Glenna and I are setting the sand dollars on the stone porch to dry when we are disturbed by the sound of a chair scraping inside.

When I go there to check, I find Mama and the Firbanks seated at the kitchen table. There are drink glasses on the lazy susan. The air is choked with tobacco smoke. Worst of all, in the centre of the table, Glenna's airline bag has been turned inside out and a number of items placed on display. *Evidence* is the word that comes to mind, when I see the look on Mama's face.

Three pairs of eyes bore in on slim, blonde Glenna, as she slips into the room behind me. I feel like a judge, or that I am about to have some terrible truth thrust upon me.

The things on the table are foreign and add to my confusion. Clothing made from animal skins. An ivory box with tiny black figures etched on the cover. A pair of high fur boots with leather laces. Things difficult to connect with Glenna in her Princess Di haircut and white sweatpants.

Like a croupier sliding a pile of chips, Mama advances an object across the table with her claw-hammer. It is a tiny, jet-black statue, with ivory accessories, minutely carved so that the stone seems to billow and fold itself into whitened creases. My curiosity aroused, I peer more closely, all too aware that Mama has engineered this moment, my discovery, my acquiescence in judgment, though I don't quite know what the judgment is yet.

There are two people, a couple — Eskimos, I can tell. The man holds a barbed ivory spear, no bigger than a pipe cleaner, with a piece of twine attached to the end. Next to him stands a woman and a dog.

My body gives an involuntary shiver. The hair begins to crawl up the back of my neck. There is something uncomfortably intimate about the statue, and familiar. The man clutches the woman's hand; the woman holds the dog on a twine leash. Their eyes are fixed on some icy horizon. They exude an air of remoteness, as though they had just stepped out of the Stone Age, from a time when the human race was younger, prouder and fiercer.

Then I see that the woman is my wife, that the carver has etched her hair to make it seem blonde, that he has captured in some crudely perfect manner her look of hopeful dignity.

I begin to sweat. This is the secret of the secret, a story carved in stone. The statue is a thing of icy beauty, a piece of shore rock, sawed and chipped and rubbed into life. Its implications for Glenna twist and swirl in my mind. Nothing holds. I have only a sense of her passion, her wonder, her unerring certitude, and the undeniable fact that she has come back, that she has torn herself away from this man, this frozen world, to return to Ragged Point.

I am only half aware of Mama as she stubs out her cigarette on a saucer and brandishes the claw-hammer. I have only time to form the words "No, Mama. No!" But the words die on my lips. With a hiss of rage, she smashes the hammer down, hitting the statue squarely, shattering and pulverizing it.

Dust and shards fly everywhere, onto the floor, the kitchen counter, the Firbanks' laps, clinking against drink glasses.

Something strikes my chest above the heart. Without thinking, I stoop to retrieve the tiny ivory spear.

In the morning, as we pack the van, an air of celebration, of dignified festivity, settles over Gulf Haven. Bubba and Effie help carry loads to the van. I have hired them to manage the place while we are gone. Needless to say, Mama is against this, but since destroying Glenna's statue she has been unusually quiet. She and the Firbanks skulk in the pine shadows by her cabin like a nest of timid, viperish snakes.

Cars have been pulling up since first thing, disgorging well-wishers. Something is happening to Ragged Point, it is generally agreed. For once, there is a feeling of hope, a feeling that things may turn out all right. The forces of love and adventure, of passion and courage and virtue are in the ascendant.

Elder Ottman returned home the day before to find his wife hunched over a stack of books on the deserts of Australia. Sheriff Buck allows that his wife, Trudy, wants to pay us a visit up in Canada one of these days. Three of the five hang-gliding mothers are pregnant again and speak of taking their unborn infants on a walking tour of Nepal before the season is out.

Glenna still does not talk much. But her silences no longer wound me. When Mama's hammer fell, I realized I too had been silent, not knowing or refusing to say the words that would unlock the secret places of her heart.

In bed last night, she told me a little about the place where we are going. The Eskimos, she said, do not use that name for themselves. They are Inuit, which means the People. For centuries they thought they were the only human beings on earth.

"When they meet a stranger," she said, "they run forward holding their bare hands in the air, shouting, 'We are friends. See, we have no knives. We mean you no harm. We are friends.'"

She said they have eighty-nine words for snow, and that in the long summer day they will stand on the shore for hours, staring out to sea. Sometimes they are watching for seals or walrus to hunt, but other times they are just staring. Itlulik, the man in the statue, also the man who carved it, is a hunter and an *anguloq*, a sort of medicine man.

"I didn't want you to find out like that," she said, holding me tight against her breast so I wouldn't turn away. "I didn't know if you loved me enough to hear me out. I missed you the whole time. He's not kind like you. Even the other Inuit don't trust an *anguloq*. I told him I had to come back and find you."

Before getting into the van for the last time, I embrace

each of my friends from the Dunkin' Donut. We are brothers, fellow unravellers of the mysteries of existence. They wish me good luck. They tell me to send back messages so that the world will seem a little more clear to them. It is a sad, yet happy, moment. Bubba dances me a step or two. Effie crushes me against her enormous breasts and laughs.

I don't know where we are going really. I have to trust the luminous stranger beside me. For courage I press my shirt pocket, where amongst the pens I carry Itlulik's ivory spear which my wife has let me keep. In my mind, I practice the words of greeting which, in my heart, I have always known.

"I am a friend. See, I have no knife. I mean you no harm. I am a friend."

# SWAIN CORLISS, HERO OF MALCOLM'S MILLS (NOW OAKLAND, ONTARIO), NOVEMBER 6, 1814

In the morning, the men rubbed their eyes and saw Kentucky cavalry and Indians mounted on stolen farm horses cresting the hill on the opposite side of the valley. The Kentuckians looked weary and calm, their hollow eyes slitted with analysis. We were another problem to be solved; they had been solving problems all the way from Fort Detroit, mostly by killing, maiming and burning, which were the usual methods.

The Indians were Cherokee and Kickapoo, with some Muncies thrown in. They had eagle-feather rosettes and long hair down the sides of their heads and paint on their faces, which looked feminine in that light. Some wore scalps hanging at their belts.

They came over the hill in a column, silent as the steam rising from their mounts, and stopped to chew plug tobacco or smoke clay pipes while they analyzed us. More Kentuckians coming on extended the line on either side of the track into the woods, dismounted, and started cook fires or fell asleep under their horses' bellies, with reins tied at the wrists.

General McArthur rode in with his staff, all dressed in blue, with brass buttons and dirty white facings. He spurred his mare to the front, where she shied and pranced and nearly fell on the steep downward incline. He gave a sign, and the Indians dismounted and walked down the road to push our pickets in. The Indians had an air of attending their eighty-seventh-or-so battle. They trudged down the dirt road bolt upright, with their muskets cradled, as though bored with the whole thing, as though they possessed some precise delineation of the zone of danger that bespoke a vast familiarity with death and dying.

The men who could count counted.

Somebody said, "Oh, sweet Baby Jesus, if there's a one, there must be a thousand."

I should say that we had about four hundred — the 1st and 2nd Norfolk Militia, some Oxfords and Lincolns, six instructors from the 41st Foot and some local farmers who had come up the day before for the society.

Colonel Bostwick (the men called him Smiling Jack) stood higher up on the ridge behind our line, watching the enemy across the valley with a spyglass, his red coat flapping at his thighs. He stood alone mostly. He had been shot in the leg at Frenchman's Creek and in the face at Nanticoke when he walked into the Dunham place and stumbled on Sutherland and Onstone's gang by accident. The wound on his face made him look as though he were smiling all the time, which was repellent and unnerved his troops in a fight.

Injun George, an old Chippeway who kept house in a hut above Troyer's Flats, was first up from the creek. He said he had seen a black snake in the water, which was bad luck. He said the Kickapoo had disappeared when he shot at them, which meant that they had learned the disappearing trick and had strong medicine. He himself had been trying to disappear for years with little success. Later, he shot a crow off the mill roof, which he said was probably one of the Kickapoos.

A troop of Kentuckians came down the hill with ammunition pouches and Pennsylvania long rifles and started taking pot shots at McCall's company hiding behind a barricade of elm logs strung across the road. We could not reply much for lack of powder, so the Kentuckians stood out in the open on the stream bank, smoking their white clay pipes and firing up at us. Others merely watched, or pissed down the hill, or washed their shirts and hung them out to dry, as though fighting and killing were just another domestic chore, like slopping pigs or putting up preserves.

Somebody said, "They are just like us except that we are not in Kentucky lifting scalps and stealing horses and trying to take over the place."

The balls sounded like pure-D evil thunking into the logs.

Someone else tried to raise a yell for King George, which fell flat, many men allowing as it was a mystery why King George had drawn his regulars across to the other side of the Grand River and burned the ferry scow so that they could not be here when the fighting started.

*Thunk, thunk* went the balls. A melancholy rain began to fall, running in muddy rivulets down the dirt track. Smoke from the Republican cook fires drifted down into the valley and hung over the mill race.

Colonel Bostwick caused some consternation coming down to be with his men, marching up and down just behind the line with that strange double grin on his face (his cheek tattooed with powder burns embedded in the skin) and an old officer's spontoon across his shoulders, exhorting us in a hoarse, excited mutter.

"Behold, ye infidels, ye armies of Gog and Magog, agents and familiars of Azazel. Smite, smite! O Lord, bless the children who go into battle in thy name. Remember, boys, the Hebrew kings did not scruple to saw their enemies with saws and harrow them with harrows of iron!"

Sergeant Major Collins of the 41st tried to make him lie down behind the snake fence, but the colonel shook him off, saying, "The men must see me." The sergeant took a spent ball in the forehead and went down. The ball bounced off, but he was dead nonetheless, a black knot sprouting between his brows like a third eye.

A sharpshooter with a good Pennsylvania Dutch long rifle can hit a man at three hundred yards, which is twice as far as any weapon we had could throw, let alone be accurate. So far we had killed only one crow, which might or might not have been an enemy Indian.

Edwin Barton said, "I dreamt of Tamson Mabee all night. I threw her down in the hay last August, but she kept her hand over her hair pie and wouldn't let me. She ain't hardly fourteen. I'll bet I'm going to hell today."

Somebody said, "You ever done it with a squaw? A squaw'll lay quiet and not go all herky-jerky like a white woman. I prefer a squaw to a white woman any day."

And somebody else said, "I know a man over at Port Rowan who prefers hogs for the same reason."

This was war and whisky talking.

We lay in the rain, dreaming of wives and lovers, seeking amnesty in the hot purity of lust — yes, some furtively masturbating in the rain with cold hands. Across the valley, the Kentuckians seemed like creatures of the autumn and of rain, their amphibian e es slitty with analysis. Our officers, Salmon and Ryerson, said we held good ground, whatever that meant, that the American army at Niagara was already moving back across the river, that we had to stop McArthur from burning the mills of Norfolk so we could go on feeding King George's regulars.

Trapped in that valley, waiting for the demon cavalry to come whooping and shrieking across the swollen creek, we seemed to have entered some strange universe of curved space and strings of light. Rain fell in strings. Some of us were already dead, heroes of other wars and battles. We had been fighting since August 1812, when we went down the lake with Brock to the relief of Amherstburg. At times like these, we could foresee the mass extinction of the whole species, the world turned to a desert of glass.

Everything seemed familiar and inevitable. We had

marched up from Culver's Tavern the day before. We had heard firing in the direction of Brant's Ford at dusk, and awakened to see Kentucky cavalry and Indians emerging from the forest road and smoke rising from barn fires behind them. Evidently, given their history, Kentuckians are born to arson and mayhem. Now they sniped with passionate precision (*thunk, thunk* went the balls), keeping us under cover while they moved troops down the steep bank.

Shielding our priming pans with our hats, we cursed the rain and passed the time calculating angles of assault. The mill pond, too deep except to swim, protected our left wing. That meant Salmon's boys would get hit first, thank goodness. Mrs. Malcolm and her Negro servant were busy moving trunks and armoires out of the house in case of fire. No one paid them any mind. All at once, we heard shouts and war cries deep in the woods downstream. Colonel Bostwick sent a scout, who returned a moment later to say McArthur's Indians had out-flanked us, crawling across a deadfall ford.

We stared at the clouds and saw fatherless youngsters weeping at the well, lonely widows sleeping with their hands tucked between their legs, and shadows moving with horrible wounds, arms or legs missing, brains dripping out their ears.

Someone said, "I can't stand this no more," stood up, and was shot in the spine, turning. He farted and lay on his face with his legs quivering. His legs shook like a snake with its back broken. The Kentuckians were throwing an amazing amount of hot lead our way.

The colonel smiled and shouted additional remarks against Azazel, then ordered McCall to stand at the elm-tree barricade while the rest retired. This was good news for us. We could get by without the mills of Norfolk; it was our bodies, our limbs, lungs, nerves and intestines we depended on for today and tomorrow.

McCall had Jo Kitchen, a noted pugilist, three of the Austin brothers, Edwin Barton and some others. We left them our powder and shot, which was ample for a few men. At the top of the valley, Swain Corliss turned back, cursing some of us who had begun to run. "Save your horses first, boys, and, if you can, your women!" He was drunk. Many of us did not stop till we reached home, which is why they sometimes call this the Battle of the Foot Race.

Swain Corliss hailed from a family of violent Baptists with farms on the Boston Creek about three miles from Malcolm's. His brother Ashur had been wounded thirteen times in the war and had stood his ground at Lundy's Lane, which Swain had missed on account of ague. Swain did not much like his brother getting ahead of him like that.

He had a Brown Bess musket and a long-barreled dragoon pistol his father had bought broken from an officer. He turned at the top of the hill and started down into the racket of lead and Indian shouts. Musket balls swarmed round McCall's company like bees, some stinging. Swain took up a position against a tree, guarding the flank, and started flinging lead back. Edwin Barton, shot through the thighs, loaded for him. Men kept getting up to leave, and Captain McCall would whack them over the shoulders with the flat of his sword.

Swain Corliss, pounding a rock into the barrel of his gun with a wooden mallet, kept saying, "Boys, she may be rough, but she sure is regular."

Bees stung him.

That night, his father dreaming, dreamed a bee stung him in the throat and knew. Swain Corliss was catching up to Ashur. He killed a Kentucky private coming over the creek on a cart horse. Then Swain Corliss shot the horse. Smoke emerged from the mill. Mrs. Malcolm ran around in a circle, fanning the smoke with a linen cloth. (*Thunk, thunk, buzz, buzz* went the balls.) Though we were running, we were with them. It was our boys fighting in the hollow. Colonel Bostwick sat on his race horse, Governor, at the top of the track.

The company gave ground, turning to fire every few yards. Martin Boughner tied a handkerchief to his ramrod and surrendered to an Indian. Swain Corliss tied up Edwin Barton's legs with his homespun shirt. Deaf from the guns, they had to shout.

"By the Jesus, Ned, I do believe it ain't hard to kill them when they stand around you like this."

"I mind a whore I knew in Chippawa —"

"Ned, I wished you'd stop bleeding so freely. I think they have kilt you."

"Yes."

They were in another place, a region of black light and maximum density. On the road, sweating with shame in the cold, we heard the muskets dwindle and go out. We saw Swain Corliss, white-faced, slumped against an oak amongst the dead smouldering leaves, Edwin's head in his lap, without a weapon except for his bayonet, which he held across his chest as Kickapoo warriors came up one by one, reverently touching Swain's shoulders with their musket barrels.

The Kentuckians had lost one dead, eight wounded and a couple of borrowed horses. That day, they burned the mill and one downstream and sent out patrols to catch stragglers, which they did, and then released after making them promise on the Good Book not to shoot at another person from the United States. The Indians skinned and butchered Edwin Barton's body, Ned having no further use for it.

During the night, three miles away, James Corliss dreamed that a venomous bee had stung him in the throat. Rising from his bed, he told the family, "Yonder, yer baby boy is dead or something." Then James Corliss went out into the darkness, hitched his horse to a stoneboat, placed a feather tick, pillows and sheets upon it, and started for the scene of the battle.

# WHY I DECIDE TO KILL MYSELF AND OTHER JOKES

The plan begins to fall apart the instant Professor Rainbolt, Hugo's graduate adviser, spots me slipping out of the lab at 11 p.m. on a Sunday. Right away he is suspicious. I am not a student; the lab is supposed to be locked. But, like a gentleman, he doesn't raise a stink. He just nods and watches me lug my bulging (incriminating) purse through the fire doors at the end of the corridor.

Problems. Problems. Professor Rainbolt knows I'm Hugo's girl. He's seen us around together. Now he's observed me sneaking out of the lab at 11 p.m. (on a Sunday). He's probably already checked to see if, by chance, Hugo has come in to do some late night catch-up work on his research project. Hugo will not be there, the lights will be out, and Hugo will be in shit for letting me have his lab key (I stole it).

Now, I didn't plan this to get Hugo into trouble. At least, not this kind of trouble. Other kinds of trouble, maybe. Guilt, for example. But now, when they find my corpse and detect the distinctive almond odour of cyanide, they will know exactly where the stuff came from, whose lab key I used, and Hugo will lose his fellowship, not to mention his career, such as it is. Let me tell you, Hugo is not going to lay this trip on me after I am dead.

Also, the whole Rainbolt thing raises the question of timing. Let us say that a person wants, in general, to kill herself. She has a nice little supply of cyanide, obtained illegally from a university research lab (plants, not animals), which she intends to hoard for use when the occasion arises.

She might, for example, prefer to check out on a particularly nice day, after a walk with her dogs along the River Speed. Perhaps after sex with Hugo — and a bottle of Beaujolais. In bed, by herself. (Hugo exiting the picture; forget where he goes. Probably a bar somewhere, with his guitar, flicking his long hair — grow up, Hugo — to attract the attention of coeds.) Her Victorian lace nightie fanning out from her legs and a rose, symbol of solidarity with the plant world, in her hand.

But now she has to factor in Professor Rainbolt and the thought that her little escapade into the realm of break, enter and theft will soon be common knowledge on the faculty grapevine, the campus police alerted, the town police on the lookout (*slender blonde, five-ten, twenty-six years old, with blue eyes and no scars — outside — answers to the name Willa*), and that Hugo will be, well, livid and break something (once he broke his own finger, ha ha).


A girl decides to kill herself and life suddenly becomes a cesspit of complications. Isn't that the way it always is? I think. And suddenly I am reminded of my father who, coincidentally, was waylaid and disarmed on his way to the garden with the family twelve-gauge one afternoon, after kissing Mom with unusual and suspicious fervour because, he claimed, of her spectacular pot roast (why he kissed her, not why he was going out the door with the gun — target practice, he said).

He was already far gone with cancer, in his brain and other places. Trying to sneak into the garden was the last sane thing he did. Can you guess that it was me who wrestled that gun from his pathetically weakened hands? That I spent the next six months lifting him from room to room, feeding him mush, wiping his ass? That in my wallet I still carry, along with other photographic memorabilia, a Polaroid of Dad in his coffin?

Let me pause to point out certain similarities, parallels or spiritual ratios. Gardens play a role in both these stories. That lab is really an experimental garden full of flats choked with green shoots. Hugo breeds them, harvests them, pulverizes them, whirls them, refrigerates them, distils them, micro-inspects them — in short, he is a plant vivisectionist. It is a question of certain enzymes, I am told, their presence or absence being absolutely crucial to something . . . something — I forget. We have made love here amongst the plants, me bent over a centrifuge with my ass in the air and my pants around my ankles, which did not seem seriously *outré* at the time. (On one such occasion, I noticed the cyanide on the shelf above, clearly marked with a skull-and-crossbones insignia.)

Gardens and suicide run in the family. Failed suicides, I am now forced to conjecture. Clearly, one did not foresee the myriad difficulties, or that fate would place Professor Rainbolt at the door as I left the lab/garden, feeling sorry for the plants — I have heard that African violets scream — thinking, why, why can't they just leave well enough alone?

The time factor is crucial. I do not relish being rushed. But when will I have another chance? Also, quite suddenly, I realize I have forgotten to find out if cyanide poisoning is painful. I have a brief, blinding vision of blue me writhing in the Victorian nightie, frothing vomit and beshitting myself. Someone would have to wipe my butt, and I, like my father, never wanted that. Never, never, never.


I see I have reached my car, our car, Hugo's and mine, a wine-coloured Pinto with an exploding gas tank. We both like to live cheaply and dangerously. Bismarck, the Doberman, and Jake, the mutt, greet me with preens, wriggles and barks of delight. It is nice to be among friends.

The dogs sniff at my purse where I often carry treats — rawhide bones or doggy biscuits or rubber balls. This time we have cyanide, which I ponder while the car warms up. The winter outside corresponds to the winter of my spirit, which is a dry, cold wind, or the snow crystals on the windshield remind me of the poison crystals in the jar.

I will be the first to admit that I have made mistakes. Once I was crossing Bloor Street at Varsity Stadium, being a cool, sexy lady without any underpants, when the wind lifted my skirt and showed my pussy to eighty-five strange men. And once I confessed to Hugo's mother about my affair with a lead guitarist named Chuck Madalone.

Hugo called this fling with Chuck an affair on a technicality. In my opinion, Hugo and I were not: a) officially going together, b) in love. I was in love; Hugo was in doubt, which is an entirely different thing. In my opinion, my date, tryst, rendezvous or whatever with Chuck (the innocent in all this) was pre-Hugo. Hugo said we (he and I) had had sex. These are his words. Hugo, like many men, appears to believe that ejaculation is a form of territorial marking, like dogs peeing on hydrants. I say, it washes off.

How was I to know, as Hugo claims, that he was in love, though in a kind of doubtful, non-verbal way, or that he would follow us home that night and spy through the window in a hideous state of guilt, rage and titillation? Hugo says "affair." I say, meanings migrate like lemmings and words kill.

Here we have, I think to myself, a jar of cyanide, which, as we who live with guitar-playing scientists know, is a simple compound of cyanogen with a metal or organic radical, as in potassium cyanide (KCN). Cyanogen is a dark-blue mineral named for its entering into the composition of Prussian blue, which I think is rather nice, giving my death an aesthetic dimension. The cyanide (in this case KCN) will also turn me blue, as in cyanosis, a lividness of the skin owing to the circulation of imperfectly oxygenated blood. Something like drowning — inward shudder.

The time factor, as I say, is crucial. I do not wish to die in this Pinto with my dogs looking on. Life will be sad enough for them afterward. With dogs, as with women, Hugo displays a certain winning enthusiasm, which is charming at the outset, though it soon wears off as he develops new interests.

I must use guile and cunning; I must be Penelope weaving and unravelling. The trick will be to secrete enough of this snowy, crystalline substance, which turns people blue, in, say, yes, a plastic cassette box, which when filed in Hugo's cassette tray will resemble in external particulars every other non-lethal cassette box. Then I can surrender the jar to Hugo for return to Professor Rainbolt with beaucoup d'apologies. I will look like an ass, but this is not new.

I carefully pour out what I consider to be the minimum fatal dose, then double it. (Oops, we spill a little — I flick it off the seatcovers with a glove.)


I dread facing Hugo, but without actually using the cyanide, in unseemly and undignified haste, there seems no way out. We are going to have a scene, no doubt about it. Hugo loves production numbers. He invariably assumes an air of righteous indignation, believing himself to be a morally superior being. This has something to do with his being a vegetarian (though a smoker — consistency is the hobgoblin of other minds) and my "affair." Which reminds me about his mother, that particular production.

How we arrived there for my first visit in the midst of a vicious quarrel over Chuck, with Hugo threatening to leave me after each fresh accusation. Now he was in love with me though doubtful if I were worth keeping. I was in tears, or in and out of them. We separated on gender lines. I went upstairs to his bedroom with his mother trailing me, all feminine concern and sisterliness; Hugo stayed with his father in the living room. His mother soothed and comforted me. She said she understood Hugo was a difficult boy (he is twenty-nine), but that we have to keep smiling, put a bright face on things.

Gullible Willa fell for this and confessed all, thinking his mother would understand and perhaps explain to Hugo that a tryst, before we were together officially, should not be regarded as high treason. You could tell that the mention of sex before Hugo upset her. Right away I sensed I had made the biggest mistake of my life (next to taking the gun from Dad's shaking fingers — that look of helpless appeal). She continued to stroke and console, but we did not pursue the conversation.

Presently Hugo, having had an argument with his father, came bounding up the stairs. "Are you two talking about me?" he shouted (hysterical). "Are you two talking about me?" His mother was frightened, or (this is my opinion) pretended to be frightened, and hurried downstairs. Thus goaded, Hugo fell to raving about his parents, treating me as a friend, a co-conspirator against the older generation. He did his usual fist-smashing and book-throwing routine. (At the peak of his performance, he will even try to destroy himself, beating his chest or thighs or temples with clenched fists. It is amazing to see and clear evidence of simian genes in that family.)

Downstairs his mother was busy telling his father everything I had revealed to her in confidence, woman to woman, about my sordid and nymphomaniacal sex life. (Chuck and I did it once, though I suppose it seemed worse because Hugo actually watched us. I did not tell his

mother this.) Next morning, when we appeared for breakfast, his father said one word, in a low but distinct voice,
then left the table. "Slut."

Clearly, Hugo had ruined any chance of my being accepted into this family as his wife. Or I had ruined it.
Living with Hugo, one begins to suspect one's own motives, actions and inactions in a vertiginous and infinite
regress of second guesses.

Perhaps I had engineered the whole thing. I confessed,
and I confess I was too trusting. Or is trust just another
moment of aggression? Very early in our relationship,
Hugo said, "I don't want to feel responsible." His theory of
psychology goes like this: behind the mind, there is another mind which is "out to get you." Sometimes it is clear
to me that I wanted Dad to live those extra six painful, humiliating, semi-conscious months. My soul is shot with evil.


The dogs cavort and make peepee as I climb the icy steps to
our apartment, lugging my suicidal burden, now ever so
slightly lightened. I compose my face into an expression of
shock and remorse. "What have I done? What have I
done?" I keep asking myself. Though I don't particularly
feel any of this, Hugo will expect it.

I walk into the kitchen where he studies (the table
strewn with graphs, print-outs and used tea bags) and
place my jar of KCN before him like an offering.

"Hugo," I say, "I wanted to kill myself. I stole this from
the lab. I would have gone through with it, but Professor
Rainbolt saw me. I didn't want to get you in trouble."

His handsome face wears an expression of irritation. I
have disturbed his concentration; I have created a situation with which he will have to deal; a situation to be dealt
with is a crisis; his world implodes, crumples, disintegrates.

He says, "It's my fault, isn't it? It's all my fault."

I am ready for this. When we were first together, I found it endearing the way Hugo thought everything was his fault — his willingness to take blame, to confess his failings. Now, after some years of experience, I realize that this is a ploy to diffuse, not defuse, the issue. By taking the blame for everything, Hugo takes the blame for nothing. Also he expects you to console him for being such a fuck-up. And sometimes you do, if he catches you on the wrong foot.

This time he doesn't catch me on the wrong foot, mainly because I have a secret agenda and cannot be bothered.

I say, "Okay, well, as I said, Professor Rainbolt saw me, so you'd better take it back. If you take it back, then he won't find anything missing. You can just say you sent me to pick up a book."

"I can't lie about a thing like this," he says.

Of course, he can't. If he tells the truth, it puts me further in the wrong. I've stolen his key, broken into the university lab and burgled chemicals with which I intend to kill myself. Not since he watched me "having sex" with Chuck has Hugo possessed such damning evidence of my inadequacy as a human being (and this time without the embarrassing question of what he was doing outside my bedroom window).

The phone rings. Rainbolt or Mama Hugo.

"Mom," says Hugo, excitedly. "I can't talk. I'm in a jam. Willa tried to kill herself. She's all right now, but she stole some cyanide from the lab. I have to put it back somehow, before she's charged!"

Charged! Now, this is interesting. Hugo intends to bring the full weight of the law to bear in his incessant battle to prove that he's right and I am wrong.

I have often wondered what he would do if he ever proved it, if he ever actually satisfied himself that it was true, because I think he needs this war of words to keep his energy up, this dialogue with me, with a woman — that's what I believe. He gets his élan, his charm with other people, from the struggle to prove himself.

But it doesn't really matter, and I drift down the hall to the bathroom, run water in the tub and pour bath salts (resembling cyanide), depressed and indolent. The problem is if I love Hugo, he slays me, and if I don't love him, it proves what he's been saying all along (just as I cannot bring back Dad, or the moment when I wrestled him for the shotgun), that I never mean what I say, that I loved Chuck to humiliate him. It's a battle of words (dialogue, duet, duel) to the death.

Presently, as I soak and pretend that I am already dead, reminiscing light-heartedly about my little stash of KCN, Hugo pushes through the bathroom door, urgent, worried and self-important. He is somewhat disappointed to find me taking a bath. Hanging from the shower head with my wrists slashed would have been better.

He says, "Rainbolt called." (I had heard the phone ring a second time.) He kneels on the floor beside the tub. "I told him what happened. It's amazing. He understands completely. His wife has been trying to kill herself for years. She's been hospitalized three times."

This is an intriguing turn of events, I think to myself, recalling a wan but gaily (bravely) dressed individual evanescing through one or two student-faculty get-togethers. Now I feel I should have paid more attention to her (me with my punk hair and skin-tight jeans and silk blouses open to my breasts), for we have something in common (and in common with Dad).

"Does Professor Rainbolt play the guitar, too?" I ask, watching my nipples float above the iridescent, soapy water like twin island paradises. Swim to my little island homes, Hugo. He is looking at them, but they do not distract him; rather, he seems to be thinking he has seen them too often.

I shut my eyes and slide beneath the surface of the bath water, feel my hair wave gently like water weeds, sense a bubble tickling the end of my nose, and relax. Everything is dark and warm, and a sensuous pressure enfolds my body (except for my knees, which are above the water and feel a little chilly). I have rather hoped that death will be like this but suspect I am mistaken. And if I were dead, I wouldn't be able to hear Hugo's voice hectoring me in the distance, echoing through the tub and the aqueous elements.

It is pleasant, and there is a sense in which I even nod off. Which gives me time to tell you that I am a photographer whom no one recognizes as such. That Polaroid snap-shot of Dad in his coffin was my first inspiration and the ideal of compositional clarity toward which I have been striving ever since. For money I wait on tables at a chicken restaurant. Because I can't get anyone to look at my photographs and I work in a chicken restaurant patronized by undergraduates, Hugo often slips into the error of believing I want to be a chicken waitress and not an artist.

". . . therapy," he says, plunging his arm into the bath water and hooking me up by the shoulders. I am mildly irritated at the interruption but truthfully cannot tell how long I have been under the water, years maybe. He looks exasperated, yet faintly self-righteous; he has just saved a chicken waitress from possible drowning.

"For heaven's sake," I say. "I don't need therapy. I don't want to turn into Mrs. Rainbolt. Evanescence is not my preferred mode of existence."

Hugo pounds the lip of the tub with his palm, a preliminary to chest-thumping. He doesn't like it when I carry on conversations like this, jumping ahead, bringing in thoughts I have had on my own. He will never understand my intuition about Mrs. Rainbolt. I have only seen her briefly and, at the most, once or twice; and perhaps I am thinking of an entirely different woman, though that has nothing to do with what I know I know about her.

Hugo lives in a world of progressive rock, vegetables and plant molecules. He loves rules. Every riff, every experiment, is controlled and conventionalized, though clearly he believes he is, and the world sees him as, a person on the cutting edge of — choose one and fill in the blank: chaos, nature, knowledge, genius, protein deficiency.

Bismarck runs into the bathroom, making a dog face when he tries to drink from the tub. For a dog with such a killer reputation, he is timid and a clown. I giggle and splash him a little, and he slides on the tile floor trying to escape. Hugo loses his temper and rips his shirt open, popping buttons into the bath.

Then we adjourn, after I pause for drying, to the bedroom where Hugo lies on the bed staring at the ceiling. He says nothing while I dress, won't even look at my body (too familiar, functional). Only grunts as we throw on our coats, collect the jar of cyanide and head outdoors to the car with a warm avalanche of dog on the stairs behind us.


Hugo drives. He usually drives when we're together. It's all the same to me, and now especially he feels it's his prerogative. A woman who commits crimes and tries to kill herself automatically loses her ability, ever shaky at the best of times, to perform simple everyday tasks like, say, driving a car. The dogs, now sensing a fight, cower in the rear, pretending to sleep. I try to remember the exact shade of blue

Prussian blue is and wonder if I would look good in that colour. Perhaps I should dye my hair.

We are about half-way to the university when Hugo suddenly pulls into a Wendy's parking lot and stops the car. For a while he stares over the steering wheel into the snow which is beginning to pile up and melt on the warm metal above the engine. Clearly, he has thought of something to say, and I wait patiently as I know I am supposed to.

"Is this all of it?" he asks, enunciating carefully, without looking at me.

"Sure," I say. "I may like the stuff once in a while, but I'm not an addict."

Hugo smashes his fist down on the dash and a cassette ejects from the player. This kind of humour is subversive and he doesn't like it. Male humour is based on the stupidity of women. I have to grab my ribs beneath my coat to keep from laughing as Bismarck sniffs the cassette between the seats.

Actually I don't feel like laughing, but my nerves are frayed and I am tired. My bath has not been a success. And, though I affect stoicism vis-à-vis Hugo's temper, his violence, his imprecations, I am quivering inside. I have failed at the simplest of human activities, dying. It seems proof of a deeply engrained and amazing incompetence on my part, an incompetence reinforced by my lack of artistic success and the chicken-waitressing, all emblems, signs or icons of my earlier lack of shrewdness and foresight when I stopped Dad from killing himself.

I am not surprised that Hugo suspects me of hiding a portion of the KCN for future use. He is used to sifting possibilities in a rational (some would say irrational) manner, used to making lists of might-have-beens. What might we have become if four things had gone right: if I hadn't prevented Dad from killing himself, if I hadn't misunderstood

Hugo's doubt, if I hadn't slept with Chuck, if I hadn't told Hugo's mother? And he thinks I am devious (right from the start — sneaking off with Chuck — though we didn't sneak, it was a date).

The worst thing is that I am wondering if I am doing this all myself, manipulating Hugo into a position that is an analogue of my own ten years earlier. Or, have I simply become my father in order to punish myself? I seem to be drifting into a phantasmagoria of analogies or substitutions (or myth or psychology) where only the verbs remain constant and the nouns and modifiers are interchangeable. For Hugo, I am clearly often his mother, or previous girlfriends; we fall in love, I think sometimes, in order to get even.

My sense of guilt increases as I recall how much I love Hugo, when I remember the gentle, loving man he wishes to be, when I think of his multiple talents and his struggle to be a musician (the scientist/musician thing induces a kind of schizophrenia in Hugo, a doubleness with its own hierarchy of substitutions). There are times when, in confusion, he lets you see this. Then you want to rush up and hold him and let your pity wash over him. When we are at our best, Hugo and I, we share this sense of dismemberment or dis(re)memberment, a sense that the beauty and magic are gone. (This is my explanation of Original Sin. Men have invented whole religions to divert themselves from this germ of self-doubt. They are an amazingly industrious sex.)

Just then Hugo makes one of those intuitive connections he is so good at but which he distrusts in me. He's been eyeing the cassette that has just popped out of the player, thinking. Suddenly he looks at me, surprised that he knows what he knows. Then he begins rifling through the cassette boxes till he finds one that doesn't rattle when he shakes it.

"No," I shout, but it is too late.

The cyanide (KCN — stands for twelve-gauge shotgun) scatters in the air like snowflakes. It is as if we are inside one of those glass globe shake-ups, a winter scene, couple with dogs, but the snow smells like almonds.

This is funny and scary at the same time. The cyanide rattles against the seatcovers like tiny balls of sleet or spilled salt. I hold my breath, shout "Get out!" and scream at the dogs as they lift their noses to test the air. Hugo, startled, watches the falling KCN with his mouth wide open, a somewhat suicidal expression, I think to myself.

Suddenly we are both fumbling for door handles, heaving ourselves into the open air. I am a split-second ahead of Hugo because I know what is going on. I race to the hatchback to release the dogs, screaming at them to jump out. This dramatic and violent behaviour on my part intimidates Bismarck who refuses to leave the car until I grab his collar and drag him out, whimpering and choking.


Hugo stands at the open driver's door, staring into the Pinto with disbelief. Snow sifts through the open doors and mixes with the white crystals, starting to melt almost as soon as it touches the vinyl. Perhaps he is thinking of possible headlines (AREA COUPLE KILLS DOGS IN BIZARRE DEATH PACT) or of his own near brush with extinction.

The Wendy's parking lot is silent. Though light blazes from the interior and there is a constant shushing sound of cars along the street, these seem not to impinge upon our little world. The dogs sit and shiver nervously, plainly confused and frightened.

"Are you all right?" asks Hugo. "Do you feel okay?"

He looks straight at me, into my eyes, as if to read me. I am a book he usually doesn't care to take off the shelf. Unaccountably and somewhat infuriatingly, I begin to cry.

"No, I'm not all right. No, I don't feel okay. Okay?"
I turn away, and the dogs follow me.
"Where are you going?"
"Home. I'm tired of this."

And I am tired. In the past few hours, I have broken several laws, had a fight with Hugo and failed to kill myself, not to mention thinking many desperate and ingenious thoughts to pass the time. Now, for all I know, we will never be able to drive the Pinto again. How will I get to work? How will Hugo drive to Toronto for rehearsals? What is the resale value of a cyanide-filled Pinto with an exploding gas tank? They probably won't even take it for junk. My life is a sorry and pathetic mess, and all I want to do is go home, crawl into bed and pull a pillow over my face.

Hugo runs after me and takes me in his arms. Either he thinks a hug will improve my outlook or near-death has made him horny. His cheek is cold and stubbly, rubbing against mine. Bismarck whines thinly. My nose begins to drip. I begin to lose my balance. I wish Hugo would let go because we are making a scene for people coming out of the restaurant. Suddenly I am aware that he is crying; Hugo wants *me* to comfort *him*. Who just tried to kill herself? I think, a little nonplussed. Jake chases Bismarck in a tight circle around the parking lot.

I pull away and walk back to the Pinto. With my gloves I begin to dust the snow and cyanide off the seats and out the door. I keep my scarf over my mouth and nose. Listen, I definitely don't want to die in a Wendy's parking lot. After watching for a while, Hugo walks into the restaurant, returning with paper towels which we damp in the melting snow and use to wash down the inside of the car.

It is cold, dirty work, and my hands and lips turn blue (as do Hugo's — not an effect of cyanide; this is because the body directs the blood to the major organs, the heart and brain, for example, to keep the warm). We are all cold and wet and miserable.

At length, we get back into the car and drive with the windows open to the lab (basement rec room) where I wait with the dogs while Hugo (Willa) returns the jar of cyanide (shotgun) to its glass-doored shelf (deer-antler rack). He seems to take an exceptionally long time, and I imagine him (we are creatures of each other's imagination) lost in thought, surprised and troubled, amongst the whispering plants, arrested, as it were, by the thunderous echoing whispers of things which, daily, he compels with his thoughts. Momentarily, he understands, as my father and I did, what it means to finish the sentence.

Home again, we shake our clothes outside and wash the dogs in the tub (the evening has turned into a complete horror show for Bismarck), and then take turns holding the shower attachment over each other. I keep my eyes and mouth shut while Hugo gently and carefully hoses my face, my neck and ears and hair. I do the same for him and have to bite my lip, seeing him with his eyes closed, naked, blind and trusting.

It is after 2 a.m. when we finally go to bed. We're both exhausted. Hugo curls up with his back to me and begins to snore. Bismarck's nails click nervously up and down the hallway outside our door, then he goes and curls up beside his friend under the kitchen table.

I lie awake thinking, thinking about what happened to Hugo back there by the car, what made him run after me, embrace me and weep — some inkling, I think, some intuition of the truth, that I am leaving, a truth that only now begins to spread like imperfectly oxygenated blood through my arteries and capillaries, turning my limbs leaden and my skin blue.

# THE CANADIAN TRAVEL NOTES OF ABBÉ HUGUES POMMIER, PAINTER, 1663-1680

> Bertrand de Latour describes Pommier as an artist whose paintings were all bad, although he considered himself a neglected genius.
> — Harper, *Painting In Canada*

**Envoi**

Tomorrow I embark for France on the last ship before the river freezes.

In disgrace.

The bishop has ordered it, though he was happy enough to embrace me sixteen years ago in Vendôme when, inspired by the Jesuit martyrs and an unfortunate incident with Mme de A____'s girl Alice, which was bound to get out, I begged him to send me among the savages that I might atone for my sins or perish in a state of grace.

I have with me two satchels of sketches, woodcuts and watercolours, as well as three larger works on ship's canvas, tied in a roll, which His Grace has let me keep.

Besides these, I possess nothing but my cassock, torn and muddy at the hem, and a broad-brimmed hat much eaten by rats.

For shoes the last nine years, I have made do with the wooden sandals of the Recollets. And I am much heartened at the thought of a new pair of leather ones my sister Adèle has written she will buy for me the moment I reach Paris.

I hear the watch passing the seminary gate, tracing his path along the ramparts, reluctant to be away from his fire this cool, autumn night. I pull the worn trade blanket tighter around my shoulders and crouch towards the candle. Someone shouts in his sleep.

I am forty-three and, in the nature of things, cannot expect to return to Canada before I die.

## The Voyage Out

Bishop Laval and the new governor, Mézy, were my shipmates on the voyage out, both treating me with exemplary kindness and piety.

Laval was but forty-two or -three, thin-lipped and balding, with a forehead like a dome. Much given to mystical exercises, he encouraged me to follow his example. This consisted of fasting and squatting in uncomfortable positions on the open deck in all weathers.

Mézy, a bluff, soldierly fellow, an old friend of the bishop's, often humbled himself as well by picking up sailors and carrying them about the ship on his shoulders, whether they wanted him to or not (one or two were nearly lost overboard when the governor missed his grip in high seas).

I followed Laval's regimen until my stomach felt like a prune, my legs burned and my head split; after which, I discovered that he often became quite oblivious during his meditations, so that I could go off and gnaw a piece of leathery pork while I sketched an old tar repairing sail or splicing sheets. (The bishop discouraged the drawing of sailors, sea birds, etc., on the grounds that my time would be better spent making copies of religious scenes for the edification of savages and children when we reached Canada.)

As we approached landfall, an incident occurred which surprised me and made me doubt my vocation.

One day the bishop was deep in ecstasy (or else he had fainted from lack of food) when a large herring gull lit upon the spar above him and dropped a load of dung on His Grace's sleeve.

The bishop awoke with a start and licked up the slime with relish, exclaiming to me that it was the best thing he had tasted in weeks.

I was afterward violently seasick for upwards of an hour.

## First Holy Work

They put me off shortly after at a fishing station called Sheep Death on an island at the mouth of the St. Lawrence where the curé had recently met his end at the hands of the local savages.

I rowed ashore in the ship's boat with a little pack, which contained my portable alter, wine, wafers, holy water and extra stockings, a sword at my waist and a travelling paint kit up my sleeve, where the bishop failed to notice it. I had a little paper for writing my annual letters of report to the King's minister in Paris and the papal curia in Rome, and I thought tree bark or animal skin would do for canvas till I reached civilization again.

The village Sheep Death consisted of five families far gone in debauchery, but full of good humour nevertheless. Every female above the age of twelve was pregnant and possessed of a voice like a bull having its stones cut off. The men were small, bearded, coated with fish oil and carbon from the rendering fires, and addicted to brandy.

One and all greeted me with enthusiasm and then seemed to forget my presence.

I kept my hand on my sword the first two weeks, not knowing precisely what fate had befallen my predecessor.

A fellow named Fanton, whom I suspected of being a Huguenot though he denied it, took me to the place where the curé had died. There was nothing left of him but six charred ribs and a bit of jaw. We gave him a Christian burial, and I said what I could for the sake of his soul.

I did eight sketches of Fanton's wife as the Virgin, in a shawl made from an old sail, with the latest of her fourteen children at her tent-like breast for the Christ-child.

For the first month, I swam in the ocean to keep clean, but as the weather closed in, I abandoned myself to the filth of the place and became a haven for eight varieties of insect life.

There being no church or manse, I bedded in a shack with the Fantons, usually with five or six children draped over my body for warmth, the husband and wife grunting disgustingly a yard or two away.

I drew up plans for a little chapel on a piece of birch bark and got Fanton to organize the men for the building, a project which was greeted with much public enthusiasm, but nothing came of it.

I married two couples, one with five children, the other, three.

A third couple, boasting no less than seven offspring, swore they were married, though I knew they were not. When I taxed the wife with her sin in the confessional (at other times used as a toilet in foul weather), she admitted to an earlier union with a man in France who she thought might be dead. Even so, her Canadian lover refused to marry her on the grounds that it might force her unwittingly into bigamy, a sin, he believed, as much frowned upon in the Bible as murder or eating beef on Friday.

I became suddenly depressed listening to her babble

and dismissed her with a penance of five Hail Marys and one Act of Contrition, which earned me a reputation for being overly lenient.

During the idle winter months, the men traded brandy for furs with the local savages, a practice strictly forbidden by the Church, on pain of excommunication, and by the King, on pain of death.

When the Indians were drunk, they traded their weapons, their clothes, their wives and their children for more liquor. The men of my parish being given to venery, there were many half-breed children in the Indian camp. Some wandered back and forth half-naked between their white and red families.

Indeed, it was not uncommon for me to wake in the morning to find some lice-ridden savage child with its arms wrapped tightly around my neck and snot dribbling into my cassock.

The savages painted themselves with red ochre, then pranced around naked as though they were dressed in court finery. It was a repellent sight, but I made many an interesting sketch of it.

In order to cleanse my mind and render myself worthy of the death I was certain awaited me the next summer at Québec, I tried to fast and meditate as the bishop had instructed. But my bowels seized up and gave me the most painful hemorrhoids which Mistress Fanton soothed with the application of a savage remedy and some incantation in the native tongue.

In the spring, I was relieved by the first ship from France (five ship's officers contracted lice from the circumstance of my sharing their cabin) and left the place, I failed not to believe, far better than I found it.

## Québec

Québec, the capital of the country, was a hamlet of seventy mean houses and about four hundred Christian souls, with as many savages sleeping in the streets. On the rock above, Bishop Laval had built his seminary, the Ursulines their convent, the governor his palace and Jean Boisdon his tavern.

The bishop met me at the pier, but soon went off with eight Jesuits new from France, who were on the same ship.

Later, he saw me in the seminary library and greeted me as Pierre. He said he had heard great things of my mission in Sheep Death (this seemed strange, as I thought myself the only person to come out of that place in a year).

He noticed me scratching an armpit and smiled. Drawing up his robe, he showed me a veritable hive of insect activity on his privy parts.

He then strongly urged me not to turn or change the straw on my pallet as this might accustom my body to unwonted ease.

We were getting along so well, I took the opportunity to ask the bishop if I might paint his likeness for the Hôtel-Dieu, wherein it would serve as an inspiration to the sisters, the sick and the poor.

The bishop said no.

Notwithstanding His Grace's instructions, I hired the bathtub at the rear of Jean Boisdon's establishment and took there a fine dinner of turnips, salt pork and dried crab apples, while his wife boiled my clothes.

I became drunk on cheap trade brandy and said a requiem mass for the poor dead mites which floated about me in their hundreds. (Later, Bishop Laval heard of this by some spy, and it was marked down as one of the reasons for my exile to Boucherville.)

I also sketched Boisdon's servant girl as Mary Magdalene, with her bodice uncovered and half a dozen angels looking on.

The town was in a mood of religious exaltation with half the populace expecting martyrdom at the hands of the Iroquois every night and the other half drunk with terror. War parties haunted the woods and byways and crept into the town under cover of darkness to murder and kidnap. Every cabin had a small cannon and a statue of the Virgin.

I carried my sword again, though the bishop disapproved. I explained to him it was not so much to protect myself as: 1) to make the savages bethink themselves before they brought upon their heads the terrible sin of priest-killing, and 2) to give myself an opportunity to escape should they happen to fall upon me whilst I was not in a fit spiritual state.

(I recall one alarum when we took refuge in Notre Dame — there were five men in the rood loft before the holy sacrament preparing to die and Arlette Boisvert at the door with an iron fry pan — but this is getting ahead of my story.)

I went to visit Governor Mézy whom I found alone in his apartments suffering from the grippe and in a chaotic state of mind.

He and Bishop Laval had disagreed. Mézy was under threat of excommunication for discharging the bishop's friends from the governing council, which, he said, was made up of frauds, profiteers and illegal traffickers in beaver hides. The bishop had accused Mézy of being a Huguenot, a Jansenist and an illegal trafficker in beaver hides.

Upon investigation, Mézy had discovered that Bishop Laval and the Jesuits themselves were trafficking in beaver hides. For a man who had been wont to carry sailors about the deck to humble himself before God, it was a bitter draught.

Hearing of my visit, the bishop ordered me to preach a sermon against Mézy in the pulpit the following Sunday as a test of my loyalty. The look on the governor's face as I proclaimed his sins and listed the torments he would suffer in Hell as a result has haunted me ever after. He does not know it, but I continue to pray for the old soldier to this day.

I was assigned to teach Latin and logic at the seminary. The students were mostly boys from the local seigneuries, rude, stupid and over-fed. Farting during the recitation of declensions was considered by many to be the height of wit.

Though these boys were especially selected by the parish authorities for their religious aptitude, I never observed any but the most grudging respect for Our Lady and her Holy Son. Most left school before they were fifteen to marry girls in advanced states of pregnancy. The rest ran away to the forests to trade in beaver hides.

One boy, Boisvert, could draw somewhat and became a favourite of mine. (The Boisverts were an old Québec family, having been there upwards of eight years.) In my spare time, I taught him the rudiments of figures, composition, Christian and heroic symbolism, etc.

Shortly thereafter he was expelled from the seminary and sentenced to the stocks for making a series of sketches of an Ursuline nun named Thérèse de la Sainte-Assomption being ravished by the Flemish Bastard, a noted Iroquois chieftain. Boisvert rendered the sketches on birch bark scrolls which he sold at five sous apiece to his classmates.

Though my role in this affair was concealed from the general public by the good offices of the bishop, I was enjoined to refrain from practising my art and given a severe penance which consisted of two hundred Hail Marys to be said while standing up to my thighs in an ox midden.

His Grace further ordered me to cease bathing, which occasioned much surreptitious delight amongst my remaining students.

### Martyre des Pères Jésuites chez les Hurons

Notwithstanding the bishop's command (he no longer spoke to me, or recognized me in public, though I would see him nearly every day in the street), I soon received my first major commission. This came from the Hôtel-Dieu Sisters who, by the vagaries of gossip, received the impression I was the artist responsible for young Boisvert's Ursuline scrolls.

The sisters wanted a large, suitably inspirational canvas for the chapel wall, depicting the deaths of the Jesuit brothers at the hands of the savages.

I set to work immediately on a piece of sail cloth, mixing my own paints as best I could and using the back room of Jean Boisdon's establishment as a studio.

A Huguenot hog gelder named René Petit had taken up residence in the back room while he plied his trade in the farms roundabout. A muscular fellow, with a Roman nose and cruel eyes, he modeled for me as an Indian brave.

Jean Boisdon's chambermaid, Paulette, stripped to the waist, with her skirts tucked up between her legs, did nicely for Indian maidens in the background.

For the martyrs, I painted myself as Brébeuf, using a small hand-mirror Boisdon kept by the bathtub. Boisdon posed as Lalement, showing, after consuming half a flagon of arak I was forced to purchase for the company, a remarkable talent for rolling his eyes and heaving out his chest in a counterfeit of agony.

Later he told me arak gave him gas.

Thrown constantly together in their work with me, René and Paulette conceived a sudden, immoderate passion for one another, which ended in Paulette becoming pregnant and demanding to be married. With the painting only half-done, René ran away to live with the savages.

Meanwhile, the studio was still in use as a bathroom, so that customers were always coming in to use the tub whether I was painting or not. (Boisdon charged ten sous for clean hot water, eight for moderately warm water used only once, and so on.)

Word got abroad about my work-in-progress, and I soon became a source of entertainment for the local drunks and bawds and trappers come to town to sell beaver hides.

The latter were often thunderously abusive, roaring with laughter at my woodland settings, my savages and the horrific poses of my martyrs — thus several well-meaning inaccuracies were avoided, including classical Grecian elements (amphorae, Macedonian lances and leg armour, a lyre, Ionic columns in front of the longhouses, etc.) which I had unwittingly imported into my representation of native life.

It was in this way that several of Québec's least respectable citizens made their way into my painting of the holy martyrs.

And, though I believe they enhanced the liveliness of the scene, the result was that the Hôtel-Dieu Sisters recognized two prostitutes, the Huguenot hog gelder, and a man under sentence of death for killing his wife and running away to the forest to trade in beaver hides. This man, who modeled for the wise, old sachem in the top right-hand corner, was arrested, tried, hung, cut down before he died and castrated, then burned to death in the Lower Town.

The whole of Québec society turned out for the occasion with a festive air. Two young ladies fainted straight away at the sight of the condemned man's mutilated body, and afterwards made a show of needing to be carried thence by several gallants who made a sort of invalid's litter with their arms.

The sisters refused to pay for my work, which was confiscated by the bishop. Later, they begged it of him at no charge and had gowns and pantaloons painted over the naked members by one Michel Lemelin, a plasterer who owed them money for medical care.

I never saw the painting again.


**Mistress Arlette, a Shameful Interlude**

I was bitterly disappointed, as you may guess, having found Canada a poor place for an artist to make his way.

I began a period of spiritual decline and excessive drinking. Turning my face from God, I often borrowed money from my students or robbed the poor box to buy the cheap, watered trade brandy which the Jesuits exchanged with the up-country savages for beaver hides.

Several times the night watch discovered me asleep in the gutter, curled up between a couple of snoring braves, with my robe over my face. It was only their affection for me and the belief, happily common in the town, that I was an artistic genius, which kept them from reporting me to Bishop Laval.

That fall, Governor Mézy, ever more scattered in mind and suffering a theological distress, went on a pilgrimage to Ste-Anne-de-Beaupré, crawling the whole way upon his knees whilst clad in his armour. He died the following spring and was buried in a pauper's grave.

His former friend, the bishop, took no notice.

The Iroquois sent a mission to Québec to sue for peace, then killed a farmer named De Lorimier in broad daylight. The new governor tried three soldiers for murdering an Indian and hanged them from the wall by the city gate. The savages were appalled at what to them seemed a wasteful and barbaric punishment. They said they would just as soon have had an apology and some brandy.

A comet appeared in the sky in the shape of a blazing canoe. Everyone agreed it was a difficult sign to interpret.

My former student Boisvert, now aged seventeen, unemployed, and the father of two, picked my pocket during the procession on the day of the Fête-Dieu.

At my request, he was whipped in the Upper Town, then marched to the Lower Town and set up again.

When it was over, I was so horrified I fell on my knees before him and begged his forgiveness. Later I lent him my cloak to hide his wounds, which afterward I never saw again, Boisvert having disappeared into the forest to live with the savages.

(It was difficult to blame the young men for thus liberating themselves from the yoke of wage work in the company warehouses, the drudgery of clearing the land, or the hectoring of their young wives. In the forest, they lived the lives of nobles in Old France, hunting large mammals for food and debauching Indian maidens, who were, I was told, nubile and complaisant.)

I took to visiting Arlette, the young man's abandoned wife, to offer her the consolation of my ministry, not to mention taking the price of the cloak out in hot meals served close to the fire.

She was a fat, depressed woman with a nose like a

knuckle — but her desire to serve the Lord was ardent. She told me how she volunteered without a second thought to come to the New World when the religious nature of the settlement was explained to her (though I have heard certain malicious tongues say it was because of the prospect of a forced marriage).

There was but one other artist in the colony at this time, a Jesuit missionary to the Iroquois called Father Pierron, a favourite of the bishop's. Mother Marie de l'Incarnation (a pious woman, a letter-writer and a wonderful lace-maker, a skill not often found in these rude parts, with a wen the size of a duck's egg on her chin) was wont to go around saying, "He preaches all day and paints all night." Which made me ill to hear.

Pierron specialized in miniature scenes, mostly genre pieces illustrating the vices and the virtues, Heaven and Hell, the Temptation of Eve, and so on, which he used for Bible classes among the savages, who were apparently much illuminated on this account.

My triumph came upon the death of Sister Marie-Catherine de Saint-Augustin in the Hôtel-Dieu. (She was a nun famous for the production of miracles: on February 4, 1663, while working in the hospital, she had seen four demons shaking Québec like a quilt with the Lord Jesus restraining them; a year later, she converted a recidivist Huguenot with Brother Brébeuf's charred thigh bone.)

Apparently, she had admired my *Martyre des Pères Jésuites* which reminded her of the great paintings (Raphael, Guido Reni) that hung in her father's house in Rennes. (Also Father Pierron was out of town.)

At this time, I was undergoing treatment — a decoction of sassafras being a sovereign specific, according to the savages — from an old, Christianized Tobacco Indian named Nickbis Agsonbare, for an ailment I had contracted from Jean Boisdon's servant girl.

The Hôtel-Dieu concierge found me fast asleep on a pile of young Boisvert's illegal beaver hides in a corner of Arlette's kitchen (though it was midday and hot as Hades, with the weather outside and the brick-faced mistress sweating over her bake-oven — the hides stank atrociously).

I had not painted for upwards of a year, my classes had fallen off and I had said mass but five times. The sole upshot of my labours since the *Martyre* set-back was the fact that the Boisverts were soon to be blessed with a third child, a circumstance which delighted everyone since the government had embarked on a system of royal grants for the fathers of large families.

Sister Marie-Catherine had been dead a week when I was summoned. She was dry as a nut and a sickening shade of gray-green, with her old white hair hanging in ribbons. I had to work quickly for the smell, and used my imagination liberally.

For once I had access to the best brushes and paints to be found in the colony. The concierge kept me supplied with cognac (I was once nearly caught napping with my feet upon the coffin lid). And I finished in two days, with only an hour or two for sleep.

After the funeral, I stayed on at the Hôtel-Dieu to add some finishing touches, a flight of cherubim, two corner scenes illustrating life among the savages left over from the *Martyre,* and a golden halo with rays.

Sister Marie-Catherine's eyes proved the most difficult test of my art (because they had been closed in death). I painted them upwards of twenty-nine times, till I gave up and bade the concierge sit for me in an attitude of prayer. I gave her his eyes, one brown, one hazel, both slightly squint, with yellow sclerae, gazing heavenward.

Mother Marie de l'Incarnation said she had never seen such a likeness. (This was music to my ears.) It was a vision, she exclaimed. On first entering my studio, she said, she had half-expected my Marie-Catherine to step out of the frame and address her (they used to call each other "little cabbage").

The sisters hung the *Marie-Catherine* in the public room at the Hôtel-Dieu where the bishop chanced to see it. I thought this would soften his heart toward me, but it did not.

Instead, I was summoned before the master of the seminary. Houssart, the bishop's valet, read a list of offences (including indolence, idolatry, blasphemy — that requiem mass in the bathtub — drunkenness and excessive personal vanity). I lost my job at the seminary and was exiled to Boucherville, near Montréal, where it was hoped curatorial duties would mend my soul, or I would find a martyr's end.


**Among the Anderhoronerons**


Boucherville was a one-year-old village of eight log hovels, a two-room, half-timbered manse for the seigneur, and a makeshift dock with the pitch still dripping from the timbers (which fell down when the ice went out in the spring), where pigs outnumbered the human inhabitants by five to one.

There were but three hundred English yards of muddy street in all, and the narrow fields running down to the river were studded with stumps as tall as a man's shoulders between which a few meagre spikes of Indian corn struggled for life.

I was much torn up leaving Arlette behind, but my good friend and medical consultant, Nickbis Agsonbare, eased the pain of departure by agreeing to remove with me.

I was also somewhat relieved to be temporarily out of

the bishop's eye, whence I had heretofore found nothing but censure and contempt, despite my good efforts to win favour.

Unfortunately, the ignorant villagers took me for the bishop's man, there being considerable jealousy between the Jesuits of Québec and the Sulpician monks of Montréal (including disputes over who could produce the best miracles).

They gave me a former hog barn ("former" only in the sense that they moved some hogs out that I might have the space) for accommodation and refused to entertain construction of a parish church until their crops were in, after which they decided it was too cold to commence extensive outside work. (I was blamed for this delay when the bishop moved me to Sorel two years later.)

Meanwhile, I discovered that Nickbis Agsonbare was trafficking in illegal beaver hides and was using his friendship with me to conceal this activity from the authorities. (After seven years in the colony, I had yet to see a live beaver — something like a large, flat-tailed rat, I supposed.)

Nickbis assured me that this was not the case, but I could not forbear remonstrating with him about the piles of beaver pelts which reached the ceiling on all sides, and I did not afterward trust him in quite the same old way.

I took to wearing an old shirt done up around my head like a turban and calling myself a priest of the prophet Mahound, but no one paid any attention.

I heard by the express canoe foreman that in my absence, a fresh, new face had appeared on the Québec art scene, a Recollet brother called Frère Luc, styled Painter to the King. In two months, Frère Luc had surpassed my total output since arriving in Canada, having already completed a portrait of the intendant and three large religious scenes for the Church of Our Lady.

All at once, painting and sketching, which had heretofore been a great joy to me, seemed tedious, nothing but daubs of colour and stark lines, without any meaning.

Nickbis, seeing my melancholy, suggested a trip to visit his in-laws hard by the Lac des Chats, or Lake of the Erie Nation, far inland.

At this time, it was a capital offence to spend more than twenty-four hours in the forest — a measure meant to stem the traffic in illegal beaver hides and keep young men from running away to the savages. Nevertheless, I agreed, scarcely caring if I was hanged or not.

We set off in June, without a word to the congregation, in an elm bark craft that would have sunk except for constant bailing with an alms bowl. For paddlers, we had Nickbis and his nephew Henderebenks, a simple-minded boy with a snapping turtle tattooed on his left shoulder and two fingers missing from his hand.

We cleared Montréal in a day and carried the canoe past the rapids at La Chine that night. Thence we threaded our way upriver through myriad rocky islands infested with black flies and mosquitoes. We saw no other human for a week, which made my heart lighten.

It is customary for explorers' accounts to include lists of wonders encountered and lands claimed for the King. I saw eight fire-breathing dragons, a tribe of elves which shot arrows at us the size of knitting needles, a giant bustard as big as a house, with a beak as hard as stone, two man-like creatures which bounced rapidly over the ground on a single leg, and a mermaid (possibly a large pike).

I claimed the following lands for King Louis: Pommierland, Pommier Island, the River Pommier, Lac Pommier, Baie Pommier, Painter's Reach, etc. (Our progress was delayed considerably on account of my insistence that we get out of the boat and put up birchbark signs to mark these geographical features.)

On the eighth day, about five leagues from La Salle's

trading fort at Cataraqui, we were captured by a roving band of Anderhoronerons who fell upon us in our sleep (we generally took a nap after lunch). There were nine of them, two old men without teeth, six teen-age boys and a younger lad of about seven years, all stripped naked, covered with grease and red war-paint against the flies, and nearly starved.

We spent two more days in camp while the Anderhoronerons ate what was left of our provisions.

On the third morning, we set out for their village, but had only gone a league or two when the little boy began to weep petulantly, saying it was his first war, and he wanted to kill one of the enemy.

The two eldest Anderhoronerons consulted and agreed to let him kill Henderebenks who immediately fell on his knees and began to sing his death song, "Woe! Henderebenks, the dancing turtle, is no more. Woe! Woe! Woe! The dancing turtle is no more!"

I gave him the sacrament of Extreme Unction, after which he and Nickbis Agsonbare fell into a theological argument as to whether the sacrament was any good without wine and wafer (these having been eaten by the Anderhoronerons).

The little boy struck Henderebenks with a stone club, knocked him to the ground, then proceeded to scalp him with a flint knife barely sharp enough to cut the skin. Henderebenks woke up part-way through the operation and resumed singing, "Woe! The dancing turtle is no more!" until one of the older boys clubbed him with Nickbis's arquebus.

Nickbis said he was sorry I had had to see this, that he hoped I wouldn't hold it against him, that really he had taken all the precautions he could, and that these Anderhoronerons were nothing but filthy savages to whom his people would never have given the time of day.

After a five-day forced march, we reached the main Anderhoroneron village or "castle" (a pleasant little town of thirteen bark-covered sheds or longhouses, with a sort of picket fence all around) where a young, wolf-clan widow named Sitole adopted me to replace her late husband. Sitole took my tattered cassock and presented me with her husband's beaded moccasins, his breechclout, a five-point trade blanket, a bear lance, two bows, a dozen iron-tipped arrows and a complete set of polished stone wood-working tools.

The next day the clan mothers elected me to the post of civil chief, or royaneur, with the name (which had also previously belonged to Sitole's husband) Plenty of Fish.

Nickbis admired my moccasins, but said to watch out that I didn't get my paint brush caught in the honey pot, a turn of phrase I did not at once comprehend. Nickbis had been adopted by an old man whose wife had died in childbirth, leaving him with twin girls to bring up.

Indeed, as I began to get about and observe things, I came to realize that more than half the Anderhoroneron population consisted of prisoners taken in war: Passamaquoddy, Mississaugua, Nanticoke, Mahican, Winnebago, Tutelo, Delaware, Chippewa, Maqua, Cree and enough French, English and Dutch to make a small interdenominational congregation for Sunday service. The ragtag war party we had encountered at our camp on the St. Lawrence River was the entire military strike force remaining to this once thronging nation.

To tell the truth, I have never felt so welcome as I did living with Sitole among the Anderhoronerons.

I took my duties as a tribal chief seriously from the beginning, sitting up many a night before the fire, smoking tobacco and sipping trade brandy (called "darling water" or "spirit helper" by the savages), discussing local political issues with the other head men (and warrant I would have had a notable impact on their history had it not been for the language barrier which made it difficult for all but one or two of us to understand each other). Sitole's cornfields were ripening beyond the stockade and required little attention. We lolled together day after day in a nearby creek, naked under the hot summer sun. I even began to sketch and paint a little, taking classical subjects such as Leda and the swan (for which I substituted a wild goose Sitole was raising for the pot), the judgment of Paris, Venus at her bath, that sort of thing.

By the end of the second month, she was with child. (Nickbis, who was called Mother Nickbis by the Anderhoronerons, scowled at the news and said we ought to be thinking harder about escape.)

Instead, I learned to hunt, finding myself adept at tracking deer and bear in the nearby forest, though I hardly needed to as the savages were more than happy to trade me supplies of meat for portraits. These I rendered on stretched doe skin with paints Sitole helped me manufacture from herbs and minerals. By first frost there wasn't a longhouse in the village without an original Pommier hanging in the place of glory. .

At midwinter, I helped the Anderhoronerons kill the white dog and myself ate of its heart. I joined the Little Water Medicine Society, participated in the ancient dream-guessing rites and laughed uproariously at the antics of the False Face dancers.

But as the winter wore on, food became scarce. The deer no longer rushed to impale themselves upon my arrow points. Sitole was forced to cut my beloved paintings into strips and boil them with tree roots to make a soup. One by one, the old people began to die. Nickbis Agsonbare's husband was the first to go, despite my old friend's valiant efforts to keep him alive.

The last day of February, our son, Adelbert Pommier

Adaqua'at, was born. I baptized him and said mass, and we ate the last of the pictures (Venus-Sitole admiring herself in a hand-mirror) in celebration of his name day, inviting as many of the neighbours as could fit into our home to join us.

That night a stranger stumbled into the village, a half-starved white man, burning with fever and covered with festering boils. He had come, he said, because he had heard there was a Black Robe, or priest, among the Anderhoronerons, and he wished to receive absolution before dying. As I made the sign of the cross upon his forehead, I recognized the face of young Boisvert, my former student, Arlette's husband, now aged and deformed beyond belief.

The next day Boisvert died. Within a week, half the Anderhoronerons followed him. The other half fled into the forest where many starved or froze to death. Sitole went mad with the fever and drowned herself in the icy creek where the summer before we had been wont to dally. Adelbert expired in my arms one or two days later. I don't know when exactly, for I carried him about for at least a week without noticing, while I nursed the sick.

Nickbis Agsonbare and I were spared, God alone knows why.

We knelt in the centre of the village, surrounded by corpses, for two days and nights, singing our death songs to no avail. Then we set fire to the place and started off together on foot, heading west, away from New France, toward the Anderhoroneron Land of the Dead.


**Last Years: Something of Me will Remain**

The epoch of martyrs and apostles was passing. My own great works were behind me. Many of the best people I called friend were in the grave. My hemorrhoids were chronic and most of my teeth had broken off as a consequence of gravel in the native corn-meal.

Nickbis and I wandered among the Far Indians for a year (I saw my first beaver that winter near Fond du Lac, a small juvenile afflicted with mange, which was immediately clubbed to death by a local hunter and sold for a cup of inferior brandy), then made our desolate return to Boucherville.

The village had swelled to a dozen log hovels, all sinking into the spring mud at a great rate. A horde of infants, barely toddlers, the hope and future of Canada, raced shrieking up and down the street, tormenting the hogs and fighting with them for scraps of food. Raw-cheeked housewives screamed at each other over their laundry tubs.

There was a letter from the bishop waiting for me at my pig-barn manse.

Once more, His Grace complained (in that pious tone he affected), I had proved lazy and inattentive to my priestly duties. I had failed to begin construction of a church, had performed no marriages, baptisms, burials or sick-bed visitations, and had neglected to post my annual letters to the King's minister and the papal curia. I was to remove immediately to Sorel, a problem parish downriver, where I would surely learn the necessary lessons of discipline and humility.

At Sorel, I built an Indian house and sweat lodge at the edge of the village, a hermitage where I passed my days in solitude, ignoring my parishioners who I felt certain would find something to complain about no matter what I did. The bishop heard of it and had me moved again.

This happened more times than I care to remember. The years were trammelled with uprootings, forced marches and fresh failures.

It was in Sorel that I began work on a definitive French-Anderhoroneron dictionary and an illustrated treatise on native customs, with my memoirs to follow. These documents, along with my notes and sketches, were lost when a bateau loaded with my belongings foundered off the Beauport shore during a subsequent transfer.

At Ile d'Orléans, Nickbis caught a head cold and went off in a day, without a whimper.

At Lévis, I drank myself into stupors between weddings and confessions, until my health broke from too much adulterated trade brandy. Since then, I have lived on a diet of water and sagamite, a sort of Indian porridge.

(They say that God tempers the souls of artists with suffering that their works might speak to the ages. I think it more likely He means to muffle them.)

A month ago, Bishop Laval recalled me from domestic exile to paint yet another saintly corpse, Mother Marie de l'Incarnation of the Ursulines this time, my last full-scale portrait in oils while in Canada.

The mourners had just lowered the old trout into her grave and were about to nail down the coffin lid when everyone noticed a radiance emanating from within which could only have been of divine origin. Eager to record this miracle for posterity and against the Sulpicians, the bishop ordered the body exhumed and sent his man Houssart to fetch me and my paint box. (They had to consult their records to discover what distant pulpit they had last assigned to me.)

But Mother Marie had died suddenly of a gastric blockage, and I could see well enough that the illusion of radiance resulted more from putrefaction of the gut than saintliness of spirit. Nevertheless, I put onions up my nose and stretched the job out as long as possible, since His Grace rarely allowed me to visit the capital.

Working from memory, I painted Sitole naked, with her

hands upraised, in the centre of the Anderhoroneron village, with the sun shining down and a garland of lilies and marigolds in her hair. I placed Adelbert at her knee and myself next to them in my Indian clothes, my face painted half-red, half-black, the sign of the Whirlwind from which the Anderhoroneron say we are descended.

I signed it H. Pommier-Plenty of Fish.

Then I painted Mother Marie over top of Sitole in the grand manner, just the way Frère Luc would have done, with a halo like a China plate behind her wimple, a great wen on her chin, a pious squint, a bit of needlepoint in her hand and that mysterious radiance which was nothing more than Sitole and the Anderhoroneron sun gleaming through.

I blacked the background and put in a narrow cruciform window such as the sisters had in their cells, a sacred heart and a Bible on a lectern with little beaver tails for bookmarks.

It was a third-rate portrait (I didn't bother to sign it) much admired in the colony, though the bishop noticed the beaver tails, which he chose to regard as a satirical interpolation and evidence of my spiritual incorrigibility.

It was on account of the beaver tails that His Grace finally lost patience and ordered me back to France.

One evening, while I was still engaged on the *Mother Marie*, I paid a call on Mistress Arlette Boisvert and we wept an hour together for our youth (she with eight children and a ne'er-do-well shipwright she called Bo-Bo for a husband).

She had a boy, she said, who took much after me and could draw like an angel. She had apprenticed him to a stone mason, so he could learn to make his living carving religious images.

I found the boy the following day in the stone-yard next to Our Lady. He had my eyes and the long arm and leg

bones that give me my awkward, grasshopper look. I asked
to see his work, and he showed me a gargoyle he was cutting for the transept roof. Then I asked to see the work he
loved.

He gazed at me thoughtfully for a moment, then swept
the marble dust from a sheaf of drawings.

There were eight Mary Magdalenes in crayon, five or
six Annunciations, a Holy Family, an Adam and Eve in a
garden stocked with moose and beaver, and a copy of my
*Martyre*, which he said he had seen while working inside
the Hôtel-Dieu basement with his master.

All the female subjects were from the same model, a
girl just past puberty, half-Indian, by the look of her cheek-
bones and hair, with breasts like brown hen's eggs and
large pale nipples.

He himself had posed for the Adam.

# THE OBITUARY WRITER

We drifted along in this empire of death like
accursed phantoms.

— de Ségur

## 1

Aiden is in St. Joseph's, dying of head injuries. Annie has gone Catholic on me. She has quit school and taken a job at a home for retarded children in West Saint John. She works the graveyard shift so she can spend the day with Aiden. Mornings, she visits the hospital chapel for mass. I hardly ever see her.

Of all the brothers and sisters (there are a dozen O'Reillys, counting the parents), Aiden and Annie were closest in age and sympathy, though all they ever did in public was bicker and complain about one another. Aiden was the family clown, a bespectacled, jug-eared, loud-mouthed ranter, given to taunting the younger children and starting fights — though he once sang in the cathedral choir and spent a year trying to teach himself the guitar. Annie is boyish and prim. She dawdles over her makeup, ties her red hair back and gets average grades in her university courses. But like many people who spend their lives reining themselves in, she has a soft spot in her heart for eccentrics and outsiders. One always knew that if anything happened to Aiden, it would be hardest on Annie. It is also natural that she should flail about, trying to locate beyond herself an agent responsible for this terrible tragedy. I say "beyond herself" on purpose, because, of course, Annie O'Reilly blames herself for everything first. Then me.

Mornings, in the chapel, she and God are sorting all this out. But I have little hope that He will see fit to represent my side of things.

We live in a brick apartment house owned by a police sergeant who is dying of cancer. He has told me about the operation he underwent, but not that he's still dying. Maybe he doesn't know. I know because the other day, returning from the scene of a fatal car crash on the MacKay Highway, I passed Sgt. Pye directing traffic. Father Daniel, Annie's priest-uncle, happened to be driving with me. He said, "That one's not long for this world. He's full of cancer, just full of it. I've seen enough to know." I was filled with envy then for Father Dan, for his knowledge of the mysteries of not-life, for his familiarity with the endless, dark ocean on which we float.

That's the sort of wisdom I sought when I first went hunting for a newspaper job. Mostly, though, I type obituaries and make lists of striking names to use in my short stories. Mornings, I rise early and type my dreams on a table beside our bed. Annie sometimes stops by on her way between the retarded home and the hospital. She'll lean on the door-jamb, smoking a cigarette and watching me type my dreams. My habits mystify her. The minutiae of my psyche seem frivolous next to her crippled children and dying brother. She lives in a world of mythological horror. I read my dreams like tea leaves, observing the signs, the motions of the universe as they ruffle the limpid pool of the unconscious. I want to know who I am before I sink back into the inanimate. I tell her this.

I go to the hospital. Aiden is in the head-injury ward, where old men mutter, fall out of bed or walk into the hall to be tackled and restrained by nurses. Once one of them grabbed Annie from behind and tried to choke her, a mad, fragile, leaf-dry, shit-stinking man.

I stand beside her chair and say, "He's in there. He's in there practising for death. It's been a shock. He never thought about it before. There's this little man inside the bombed-out control centre with the frizzed wires and smoking lights, all dripping with goop from the fire extinguishers. He's pressing buttons frantically, trying to get a line out, panicked, not knowing what to do.

"Later, the little man will give up, collect his coat and lunchbox, wrap a scarf around his throat, turn out the lights and lock the door. Then Aiden will be dead. Where will the little man go? I don't know. Home, probably. Back to the infinite split-ranch in the sky, with three pear trees in the back yard and a tire swing for the kids, and wait for his next job. What's the little man's name? He hasn't got one. But he's all there is."

Annie stares at me as if I were crazy; she prefers to pray. Aiden is taking it about as calmly as anyone, sleeping it off like a hangover. Life.

Old Mrs. Lawson who lives on the floor below persists in leaving her door ajar. She treats the landing as a parlour and has decorated it with antique tables and ornately framed prints of Saint John harbour in the days of the sailing ships, the port a forest of spars and sheets. When she hears me climbing the stairs, as likely as not she will think of an excuse to ambush me and talk. Sometimes her stove won't start — she'll tell me she hasn't had a hot cooked meal in a week. Sometimes she'll gossip about Sgt. Pye who bought the building from her after her husband's death.

Once she told me about the tenant who used to live in the apartment Annie and I share. (She insists on calling Annie "Mrs. Cary," though I have told her a dozen times we aren't married. As in, "Is Mrs. Cary still keeping those late hours? Mercy me!") It turns out that our bed was a deathbed, something I had long suspected, though for no particular reason. Frank Beamish, a retired foreman from the sugar refinery, died there in his sleep a month before we moved in. Of course, Sgt. Pye cleaned and redecorated the place, but, said Mrs. Lawson, she can't help thinking she senses "something" above her head late at night, when the distant foghorns sound.

I think of Aiden in his bed, and Frank Beamish and Annie in bed with me (yes, there is a symbolism attached to beds, those banal loci of love, death and dreams) and my strange dreams since we moved in. This bedroom of broken dreams.


Mornings, when I type my dreams, my mouth is bitter and clogged with dead cell detritus. It floats in the air. Those motes you see in the sunlight in the window. Annie used to be a sack angel — that was her revolt, everyone's really, the only thing we do to reverse the current, twisting and snapping our backs like salmon struggling upstream, against the flood of time, to spawn and die. We would beat together like fighters in a ring, like tiger-moths against the killer light, and Annie would expire, whispering, "I love you. I love you."

She was a technical virgin when we met, though she had had a lover in high school, an older girl she met playing badminton. When this girl left for Montreal to study nursing, she began writing Annie passionate love letters. Annie panicked, burned the letters, flushing the ashes down the toilet, drawing back from the aberrant entanglement, the suck and slop of emotion, the dark flow. She became prim. At a party, drunk and ironical and somewhat provoked by her coldness, I put my hand down the back of her pants and felt her ass. "I don't know what to do," she said. "Why are you hurting me?" Later, I made her bleed. "I love you," she would say, and die. "I love you."

After sex, she becomes formal, embarrassed, shy and neat, with every hair in place, her back straight. I sometimes laugh at her, laugh in her face. I say, "Abandonment is a commentary on primness, just as my dreams are a gloss on obituary-writing." She makes a sour face, reties her hair and takes an extra fifteen minutes with her makeup to drive me mad. We both understand that I am titillated by her dual nature and her lesbian past. I am a lover of paradox, of *outré* juxtapositions and jokes — this is the way we talk about death.


Across the landing, there is a single room Sgt. Pye rents to a middle-aged black man named Earl Delamare. Earl is the colour of dust, or he is one of those black people whose skin always looks like it needs a quick buff-up with Lemon Pledge. Earl lives on welfare and a disability pension for some back injury. He's unmarried. He has never spoken to Annie or me. The first week or two after we moved in, he would open his door a crack whenever we came or went — dusty skin, white eyeball. It gave Annie the shivers. She would shake her shoulders and skip out of sight, either down the stairs or into the apartment.

Now that we hardly ever come and go together, I rarely see Earl. Though mornings, when she stops by for a visit, Annie sometimes remarks that he is still there, watching. When she is cranky, she'll accuse me of being friends with Earl, or make believe we are twin brothers, or one and the same person. The truth is Earl and I don't get along well, this in spite of the fact that we have never even spoken to each other.

Nights, now that Annie's away, Earl will get drunk and stand outside my door shouting obscenities, taunting me about my lost sweetheart. I do not respond — at first, because I was afraid of him; now, because I am not afraid of him — which only infuriates Earl. He rants on the landing, getting drunker. (God knows what Mrs. Lawson thinks is going on. Perhaps this is the only "something" she senses.) He creates complex plots out of whole cloth, accusing me of devilish connections, quoting *Revelations*, speaking other names I do not recognize. He says he's going to call Sgt. Pye and have the police put an end to my racist cabal, before my friends and I burn him out. Lately, he's been going on about some mysterious group called the *Numéro Cinq*, which he thinks is holding meetings in our apartment.

I do not tell Annie any of this. Perhaps none of it's true.

I tell her, "Without someone else we cannot exist." Of course, I mean this in the contemporary sense — the Other.

She hasn't forgiven me for taking a newspaper job. Or, more precisely, she hasn't forgiven me for being content, for burrowing into the warm mud of the daily press, like an ancient fish into its river bed, and waiting. She prefers my previous incarnation as a discontented junior lecturer at the university at Tucker Park, where we met — long hair

and tattered jeans, waving my unfinished dissertation like a
toreador's cape, the student's friend. Because she cannot
bring herself to rebel, she adores rebellion in others — in
this way all love is pathological. But I have grown tired of
drawing attention to myself.

Moreover, it was her father who introduced me to the
city editor. Of course, Annie worships her father, that
gruff, taciturn patriarch. Yet their relationship is difficult,
and she yearns for independence. Her father found Aiden
jobs, too. The summer before Aiden worked on the Digby
ferry as a deck hand to earn his university tuition. But
Aiden made a show of accepting the job under duress,
with an air of knowing his father had laid something on
the line to get him hired, to which extent the father was
now in his son's power.

Aiden boasted he could always go back to cutting pulp
in the woods. But the last time he did this he nearly cut his
foot off with a chain saw. Aiden's body is an archaeology of
his experiences: the chain weal on his cheek from a fight
with a biker, the knife scars on his arm from the time he
and a friend intervened to stop a gang rape on the night
beach at Mispec, the thick diamonds of white skin on his
knuckles where he smashed his hand through the kitchen
wall after an argument with his father.

Now Aiden is dying; he's only nineteen and, though we
live together, I don't see Annie anymore.

The librarian is a fey, blonde woman named Lyn Shaheen.
She wears wire-rim glasses and has long, thin breasts of ex-
ceptional whiteness. For weeks I went to the library hoping
only to catch a glimpse of her out of the corner of my eye.
One day I screwed up enough courage to speak. I said, "I'm
writing a book, a novel, you might say. I need music to go
with it. In the text, I mean. I need something mad, some-

thing eerie." She looked at me strangely, but led me to the record collection. Mussorgsky, she thought. *Night on Bald Mountain.* Cage, she suggested. But no, experimental music would be too rational. Lyn Shaheen. I played the records. In truth, I am writing a novel. It's about a woman with epilepsy, a rare form of the disease in which the fits are triggered by the sound of music. The young woman is a concert cellist who develops seizures in her twenties following a car accident. Out of pity, her lover murders her. On subsequent visits to the library, I have told Lyn the plot of my book. We have had coffee together at the Ritz restaurant next to the bookstore on King Square. We have kissed in the street, though I was terrified one of the O'Reillys would see us and report me to Annie.

I don't want to make this depressing for you. This story does have its lighter moments. For example, Aiden lying dying in St. Joseph's has convulsions (not necessarily funny in themselves), which the doctors attempt to control with drugs. Occasionally a message fights its way from what's left of his brain to an arm or a leg and some macabre incident will ensue. Annie and I will be sitting next to the bed when, suddenly, Aiden's right leg shoots up to attention, exposing his catheter tube and waxy, shrunken genitals. Flustered, Annie will jump to her feet and try to press the leg back down on the bed. This always reminds me of those silent-movie slapstick routines. I half expect Aiden to lift his other leg as she pushes the first down, or his arms to fly up over his head, or his torso to rise.

Dying, Aiden has preserved his sense of humour. I am with him in this, considering irony to be the only suitable mode of comment on our universal disaster. I try to explain this to Annie. I try to tell her that if she would see Aiden as a different sort of symbol, she could remain in love with me, we could get back into bed together. Instead of praying to Christ, she could go back to being Christ every night.

I have always envisioned myself as the Roman soldier offering the sponge of vinegar, gambling for the robe, sliding his spear into His belly — irony, detachment and the ultimate kindness — that Roman soldier was the only interesting character in the whole drama, the only person who refused to react within the religious or political scheme of things, the only non-fanatic.

Well, I try to explain it, and she pushes me out of the head-injury ward, shushing me, whispering angrily for me to shut up, tears like jewels on the pillows of her cheeks — she has her point of view, too.


This is in Saint John on the Bay of Fundy, with its Loyalist graveyard in the centre of the city, moss covering the bone-white stones under the dark elms. City of exiles dreaming of lost Edens, it carries its past like a baited hook in its entrails. The O'Reillys, the Shaheens and the Pyes are descendants of Irish immigrants, survivors of the Potato Famine and cholera ships; Earl Delamare is the grandchild of American slaves. Beneath the throughway bridges, on a swampy waste next to the port, lie the ruins of Fort LaTour, scene of an even earlier betrayal. It's no wonder these people see themselves endlessly as victims.

The place where we live, Sgt. Pye's ageing apartment house on Germain Street in the South End, lies between the dry dock and the sugar refinery. We can hear the boat sounds, bell-buoys and foghorns in the night. When a fog blows in, as they often do, the streetlights look like paper lanterns hanging before the houses. Afternoons, when I finish work, I sometimes climb to the rocky summit of Fort Howe to watch the mist nose up through the port, threading the streets of the city like an animal trying to find its way in a maze.

Best of all is springtime, when the freshets swell the river, flooding Indian Town and Spar Cove above the falls. Television cameras mounted in chartered helicopters transmit aerial shots of a strange, watery landscape upriver. When the land dries, children set grass fires in railway cuts and vacant lots. Saint John is a wooden city, rebuilt hastily by ships' carpenters after an earlier fire. So this is always dangerous; the whole place could go up. These are the brilliant spring days after the freshets, when I take my position on high ground and watch smoke drifting over the sagging, pastel-coloured houses and hear sirens snaking through the streets and dream that everything man-made is being scorched clean, reabsorbed into rock and air.

Aiden is in St. Joseph's, dying of his head. This has been going on for three months. Annie, his sister, and I are breaking up. We are in the midst of the painful process of tearing down the lines of communication. Every time we talk it is like a fresh storm blowing a tree across a telephone wire, ice forming on the transformers, a flood washing away a cable. We are disentangling. Until all that will remain is the silence blowing like a cold wind against our faces. This is all right. You needn't worry about me. When I feel that wind, I know who I am.

Aiden is dying. He is asleep (in a coma) in St. Joseph's. He always seemed like a jerk to me, so it doesn't bother me much that he is dying. Except that his dying is contributing to our breakup. (Yes, I am jealous of a dying brother. God, how he used to irritate Annie. Once we had to rush to his girlfriend's apartment after she took an overdose of sleeping pills. We spent the night, brewing endless cups of coffee, walking her up and down. Annie swore she'd never speak to Aiden again — now, he has all the glory.)

He's suddenly moral. He's suddenly okay, with a ready-made excuse for missing mass. (Hell, they bring mass to Aiden. Those women have him right where they want him.) The story is that he got drunk (as usual) at a campus party in Halifax, tried tightrope-walking on a balcony railing and fell three storeys onto concrete slabs. The impact crushed the left side of his skull, but a surgeon kept him alive by cutting away the bone and draining the fluid build-up. That first week he nearly died a dozen times. (I was there. I was a tower of strength, escorting his mother back and forth from their hotel, playing cards and word games with his brothers and sisters in the waiting-room. Briefly, I was forgiven for corrupting Annie.)

I recall the surgeon coming to tell us pneumonia had set in, that the case was hopeless unless he suctioned Aiden's lungs hourly through the night. It was clear, from the doctor's tone, his kindness and the set of his eyes, that he was telling Annie's father: "I can let him die tonight, which would be better for everyone, or I can prolong this." But you only had to glance once at the father's face to know what his answer was. These people are Catholic; they have met the Pope. On top of their upright piano, which stands next to the TV and the police-band radio in the living room, there are back-to-back photos of John Paul II and John F. Kennedy. They toe the party line. Whatever happens, they come down blindly on the side of life.

Sgt. Pye evicts Earl Delamare. It's my fault, too, because I was taunting Earl, playing on his fantasies. It's possible I have driven him mad. One night he came to my door, first listening, then mumbling, then beginning his litany of wild accusations. Instead of responding with my usual silence, I put *Night on Bald Mountain* on the stereo. As the music rose, I began to intone the French advertisements on the backs of cereal boxes in my kitchen cupboard.

The music gave Earl fits; he practically howled with rage. "*Numéro Cinq! Numéro Cinq!*" he cried. I played John Cage on the stereo and began to read the cereal boxes backwards, imitating several voices at once. Earl began to beat the door with his fists, perhaps even his head. I could see the panels giving with the force of his blows. In the midst of this I heard Sgt. Pye climbing the stairs. When he came into my apartment, he found me sitting in an old Morris chair, eating a bowl of Rice Krispies, with the stereo low. He had a face like a yellow skull. Earl had retreated to his room, like a mole going underground. But I could still hear him shouting "*Numéro Cinq! Numéro Cinq!*" When Sgt. Pye let himself into Earl's room, the black man went through the window and down the fire escape.

After Earl's things were moved out, I sneaked into his room to look around. There were five bags of empty Molson's bottles in the kitchenette. His closet was papered with cut-out magazine ads for automobiles. On the bare hardwood floor of the bed-sitting room, under the single, naked light bulb, I found the photograph of a young black woman.

One afternoon, I stop by the library. I am on my way to Connor Street to have dinner with Annie and her family. Oddly enough, I think her father is trying to patch things up between us. Lyn Shaheen is pleased to see me. We chat by the record collection, then we meet again in the stacks, near philosophy where no one ever goes, and kiss. When I look up, I notice we are next to the Ms for Mortality, Metaphysics and Man. She has strange lips and a tongue that she runs over my teeth. I stroke her long breasts beneath her sweater. Her hair smells like old books.

I wait for her to get off work, then, for a while, we snuggle together in the front seat of her Volkswagen. I undo her pants and masturbate her with my fingers. Outside, a blizzard whirls around us, obscuring the Viaduct and the bridges across the river. Her Volkswagen is white; in all that snow, we are invisible. Without saying a word, she takes my cock in her mouth. She is the keeper of the words. She is the beast in the labyrinth. When I come, I am, briefly, nowhere, lost, swirling in a semantic ocean. Then she drops me a block from Annie's house.

There is no fiction in this story. I have, on the other hand, like any author, permitted myself occasional legitimate assumptions. I am the obituary writer. I do other things as well. But mornings I begin the workday by typing up the form obituary notices dropped in the night mailbox by representatives of the local funeral homes. The format is pretty much set in stone, and I have little leeway in the manner in which I choose to present my material. Nevertheless, I try insofar as I can to add some colour and meaning to the bare facts I have to work with.

Let me tell you, it makes all the difference in the world if you can say so-and-so died "suddenly" and "at home." Age can be a factor. From a human interest point of view, the younger the deceased the better. Death at an advanced age, say, past a hundred, elicits only a mild exclamation from the bored reader. But give me a little girl, who dies at three, and I can bring tears to the eye. Personally, I enjoy the stories of early retirement deaths. A welder, say, works all his life for a single firm (I bring in such telling details as his union affiliation, his membership in the Knights of Pythias, his forty-five year watch), then retires at sixty-five, only to die a few months later "after a brief illness." What I feel is that the obituary writer is a moralist, a prophet. Everything I type tells the reader, "All is dust; all is vanity." A salutary message in this age of rampant materialism.

Soon I will be typing Aiden's obituary. The thought, I am sure, has crossed Annie's mind and makes her uncomfortable. But these days everything I do seems to make her uncomfortable.

Aiden is in St. Joseph's, dying of head injuries. Annie shaves him, washes him, rubs salve on his bed sores, feeds him (I find this amazing — a man in a coma can be made to swallow a little Jell-O from time to time), changes his catheter bag, plays him music on the radio and reads him his favourite science fiction novels — Bradbury, Heinlein, Asimov and Wells. Sometimes, when Annie cannot be there, I go and sit with him myself.

It is curious how involved you can become in gauging his level of wakefulness. I tell jokes, insult him, instruct him to blink an eyelid, yes or no. I tell him secrets, shameful facts about my relationship with his sister, just to get a rise out of him. But Aiden is unflappable, and I quickly grow tired of the game. I recall a religious (though not Catholic) friend of mine, describing her mother's death: "The last week was difficult, you know, the terribly difficult time when the soul is separating from the body." Something like this is happening with Aiden. His existence is entirely passive, and he has lost even the sense of the sense of loss.

(It is during one of these clandestine visits that Annie suddenly appears and, in a fit of pique at finding me there — somehow this confuses the pristine relationship she enjoys with her brother, implying that, even as a vegetable, he might have a life of his own — she reveals that she has learned "everything there is to know" about my affair with the librarian.)

Two things drew me to her at the beginning: the way she blushed when she failed to pronounce Dostoëvsky correctly in my literature class, and the way, once, in an unguarded moment, I saw the pink band of her underwear show above the waist of her jeans. These images of self-betrayal, Annie's tiny pratfalls, are the imperfections in the other we attach ourselves to and which they strenuously deny and hide. These are the buds of conflict, the rifts. I have not loved Annie for that for which she desires to be loved.

I find out from Sgt. Pye that Earl is staying at the Sally Ann. In a few weeks, a judge will hold a hearing for his committal to the Provincial Hospital on the other side of the river. I buy a six-pack of Molson's and go down to see my former neighbour. He doesn't recognize me, but the beer is a fine introduction. We walk through King Square to the Loyalist Burial Ground to sit amongst the stones and drink and talk. Earl used to be a checker at the port before the new container terminal and his chronic back injury forced him out of work. He once owned a house in West Saint John, near the Martello Tower. Now his family has all moved to Halifax; his wife is dead. He's actually a good-looking man, with that dusty skin and his woolly, white sideburns.

When we finish the beer, I take a deep breath and hand him the photograph. It turns out, as I had begun to suspect it would, to be a photograph of his dead wife, a woman he loved deeply but who betrayed him with another man. I tell him I am researching a newspaper story about a secret terror organization called the *Numéro Cinq*, that I'd appreciate him telling me anything he knows about it. Earl is silent, but tears come to his eyes. I say, "I don't know much. I've been tracking them for years." Earl nods vigorously. "But they're everywhere," I say. Earl hides his face in his hands. "Everywhere," I say, "and we're doomed."

## 2

I will tell you now that Aiden dies. Perhaps you have already guessed it. Annie and I finally will have separated for good. I will have gone away to another city and another newspaper job. I will fly back for the funeral. I do this only partly because I hope to patch things up between us. Mostly it is because I like her family, her mother and father, who have often been kind to me, especially when Annie no longer loved me, and all the countless little O'Reillys. (There will, it appears, be new additions — Annie's sister, Amelia, a soft, kind, simple person, has fallen in love with a dreamer who will never support her, but has made her pregnant.)

I fly back for the funeral and book myself a room at the old Admiral Beatty Hotel. I recognize one of the bellhops, a homosexual classmate of Aiden's. I invite him for a drink in the bar when he goes off work and he tells me how the other boys used to tease him for being a sissy. In those days, Aiden was the only one who stuck up for him. Sometimes, he tells me, he thinks Aiden was the only person who was ever decent to him. I am shocked and chastened. I do not like to think of Aiden as a hero, but life always has a way of complicating itself.

I will fly back for the funeral and my faint heart will ache for the beauty of the New Brunswick forest as we descend through its autumnal aura. I will see the pulsing veins of its rivers and the gashes of civilization and the encroaching, all-blessing forest, and know that I too am only temporary, that this fever will pass, that the universe is only a bubble of my dreams.

I will take a taxi to the funeral home. I will see Aiden cradled in his coffin, so very thin and frail, not at all the laughing boy I remember, not mischievous at all, but thin and gaunt, with his skin sunk down into his cheeks, and so small it seems even his bones have shrunk. Eleven months he will have been dying, eating Annie's Jell-O, listening to her lover's words.

Aiden's mother will sit by his head in mournful majesty. For a woman who has borne ten children, she is remarkably beautiful, possessed of a serenity I have always envied. I will kiss her cheek and say my say. And shake his father's hand. They will call me Flip in the old way. Annie will not be there — away somewhere, they tell me, sacrificing herself, cooking for the wake. (It is clear to me suddenly, as it must be to everyone I speak with, that I have been desperately in love with her all along.) Nights, her eldest brother says, after the public hours, she comes and sits with him, talking and talking, as if he understands. Aiden, the world. It will seem so strange, the terrible present, the irretrievable past. The world is not supposed to be this way, I will think to myself. The world is not supposed to be like this at all.

I will fly back to Saint John for the funeral. I will have written other stories about the place. I will have made fun of it — the Loyalists, the Reversing Falls, the petty pride. I will have had some vengeance. But when the time comes, I will want to go back. I will always want to go back.

After the viewing, I will take another taxi to visit Lyn Shaheen in an out-lying village called Ketepec, where once

(I recall) when I as a reporter, a black bear stumbled out of the woods and was shot to death. She will have married a man in a wheelchair, a man she knew before she met me, a man she returned to because I hurt her. Because I will feel badly about myself, because things have all gone downhill for me, I will try to kiss her when she goes to make coffee in the kitchen, out of sight of the man in the wheelchair. And to my surprise, she will kiss me back, running her tongue over my teeth, licking my face, searching with her fingers between my legs, finding that which she only half-wishes to find, the instrument that offers yet separates us forever from ecstasy.

The next afternoon I will walk the gritty streets from the hotel to the funeral home in silent despair. Annie meets me at the door; she shakes my hand. It is clear that I am nothing to her. And her grief is practical, not mythic as I had expected; she has done with wailing. But I am happy enough just to be near her. Going to Aiden, she proved I could not satisfy her, or that she did not wish to be satisfied, that she had accepted some sad truth about hunger and miracles.

Leaving the family for the closing of the coffin, I head up the hill toward the Cathedral of the Immaculate Conception, where the funeral mass is to be held, Father Dan officiating. But at the last moment, as I climb the cold, granite steps to the door, I turn aside like one accursed. Instead of waiting for the O'Reillys, I climb further up the low, clapboard canyons of the city to Carleton Street, past the stone Anglican Church, and turn down Wellington toward Germain Street and the South End.

Mrs. Lawson is alive and pleased to see me again. ("And how is Mrs. Cary?" she asks, oblivious to my personal misfortune. Because I am wearing a suit, she thinks I have come up in the world.) Sgt. Pye is dead. Some anonymous corporation has bought the building from his widow, and Mrs. Lawson is in danger of running through her tiny savings to pay the rising rent. Also, the new landlord has made her take in her tables and shipping prints. She tells me that Earl Delamare has been released to a half-way house in West Saint John.

It takes me half an hour to get there by cab, what with a stop along the way to buy beer. (We drive over the Reversing Falls Bridge, with its fine view of the mental hospital and the Irving pulp-and-paper mill.) Earl is watching television with a number of other depressed-looking people. At first he doesn't recognize me (he has a difficult time just tearing his eyes away from the TV screen), but I finally convince him to take a walk through his old neighbourhood. (A social worker confiscates my beer at the door, so the first thing we do is head for the nearest liquor store and buy a fifth of Johnny Walker.)

We walk in silence until we reach Earl's former home, the seat of his many sad memories. There is no one around, so we walk through the yard, peering into windows, eyeing the shrubbery that Earl planted many years ago. For a while, I sit on the grass, drinking from a brown paper bag, while Earl does a little weeding and tells me what it was like to be newly married in this snug little house. The cheerful, domestic tales he tells have the quality of dreams frozen in time.

When a neighbour comes out to ask us what we are doing, we move on. We stop at the Martello Tower (built in 1813 against possible attack from the United States; during World War II, there were anti-aircraft guns mounted on the roof) to admire the sweep of the river, the harbour and the roofs of the city beyond. Earl points out the old shipping-sheds, where he used to work, and the new container port with its vast spidery cranes. A chilly wind is blowing off the bay, bringing with it little runners of mist.

As we swing down St. John Street toward Dufferin Row and the Digby ferry landing, we turn up our collars for warmth and drink deeply from the bottle. We joke about taking a return trip on the ferry, drinking our way to Digby and back in the ship's bar. Earl is in an upbeat mood, and, to my surprise, I find my own spirits beginning to rise. But the ferry slip is empty, and we change plans in mid-stride, heading past the gate and plunging down to the empty shoreline.

The tide is out. The beach is strewn with bits of driftwood twisted into anguished forms, rusty pieces of machinery, shards of coloured glass and cobbles worn smooth and round by the action of the waves. We pick our way carefully toward the headland and the breakwater that stretches away from it into the fog. We shiver in the heavy, moist air. Just past the foot of the breakwater, we come upon an abandoned concrete bunker, built to protect the harbour from the threat of German U-Boats.

Dusk is falling, but we can no longer see the lights of the city for the fog. We are conscious of the city, rushing with cars and people (in spite of everything, I have not forgotten Aiden's funeral), just across the cold, gray water, but we are temporarily isolated from it. As we sit huddled together against the bunker wall, peering at the point where the breakwater disappears, it is as if we have entered some other alien, yet beautiful, universe.

# TURNED INTO A HORSE BY WITCHES, PORT ROWAN, U.C., 1798

## 1

Old widow McMichael is one.

I set a trap at the foot of my bed, a contraption of beams and pulleys bolted to the floor. It has nearly been the death of me, twice. Oncet my wife's dog Sally got her paw caught coming to wake us in the morning.

Sometimes we wake up and there is the tell-tale smell of ashes and urine all over the cabin.

I believe there are certain precautions everyone should take. Never marry your daughter off on a Friday nor make soap when the moon is turning. Plant your cucumbers in the second quarter if you want pickles for the winter. I keep a good supply of horseshoes about the place.

Oncet I had my gun and was climbing the ravine to hunt deer, when I espied Mrs. McMichael on the path ahead of me. The dog whimpered and would go no further, so we came home. The dog has never run a deer since. It is well known that witches will ruin a good dog by peeing up its nose.

## 2

I am a medical man. I had a practice in Philly that was ruined by the rebels and you-know-who. After the war, they took my house because I would not say the oath of allegiance. Dr. Rodney has it now, but I saved my bag and walking-around instruments.

I rowed all the way from Niagara with the wife, a cow and eighty apple trees wrapped in burlap.

The sunlight off the lake is hot and bright, and the water looks like quicksilver. Sometimes you cannot tell where the water ends and the sky begins. The first winter ice blew up off the lake and killed half my orchard. Indians took the cow, but I believe it was an honest mistake.

At first there were no other white people and even now my practice is extended.

The wife has given birth to a son, who is whole, which is lucky considering the evil we have been through.

### 3

We are for Henry Alline and the New Lights.

When he was eight, my boy fell into a trance in a field, trying to save a cow that had hung herself on a line fence — a clear case of witchery. I nailed him a box, and the wife prayed and aggravated over him for three days, after which he sat up and asked for a sup of maple syrup candy.

I was about to wallop him with a fence paling, when he espied Elder Culver on his knees at the foot of the box and cried out that he had been in Heaven talking to angels. He begged Elder Culver to baptize him and let him witness for the Lord at the next camp meeting.

The wife said, Praise Jesus and don't beat the boy.

Prior to this, the boy had shown little inclination toward theological subjects.

### 4

Oncet I woke from a nap to see a young girl in a white shift, strolling in the orchard.

When I approached, she turned to greet me with a shameless invitation. I could see her tiny breasts and nether hair through the cloth of her shift. With a cry of dismay, I realized I had left my Bible on the table.

She made me mount behind her on a fence rail, and we flew across the lake to a place called Dunkirk, where she changed me into a horse and tied me in a stable. Through chinks in the stable wall I saw a hundred witches cavorting with the Beast around a roaring fire.

They brought me water in a bucket and fed me oat straw and carrot greens.

When I awoke I was in my own bed and the wife said I had been there all night.

But I shit oat straw for three days and my digestion has not been up to much since.

## 5

I am old now. The wife has been called to her reward and is buried under a rock in the orchard.

My boy had four sons — John, David, Michael and Cornelius — and five daughters — Elizabeth, Sophronia, Catherine, Susannah and another whose name I cannot recall but who married Edward Bowen.

My boy is a blacksmith and a deacon in the Baptist Church. In 1802, they made him constable of Walsingham. For a person who spoke face-to-face with the Lord when he was eight, he has not amounted to much.

I like the one who married Edward Bowen the best. She is named after her grandmother.

The McMichael place has been empty twelve years and there are raccoons in it.

Before she died, the old widow fell into the habit of walking to my yard gate and waiting for me to espy her. I believe she derived some pleasure from my terror and stuttered imprecations.

There are no witches in Norfolk County now. They have cut the forests down and killed the bears, and Scotch shopkeepers have covered the land like a blight. Whisky has come into disrepute. And there are too many men and women like my boy, people of middling stature who have the Lord's ear.

# A MAN IN A BOX

## 1

A woman followed me home to my box today, claiming to be my wife.

I did not recognize her.

According to notes gummed to the wall of my box (n wall, ur quadrant, very early notes scribbled in a vehement hand on curled and faded yellow stick 'ems — vestiges of an earlier denizen, no doubt, unknown to me personally), there once was a wife who abandoned her husband (referred to as "I," "me" and "the innocent in all this") for the manager of a Toys R Us store in Paramus.

This is the only reference to a wife I can find in any of the texts affixed to the cardboard walls of my home. It doesn't seem possible that this is the same woman. I don't even know what a Toys R Us store is, nor have I ever been to Paramus.

The woman seemed distraught. She tried to speak with me. But I have a policy against addressing people I don't know personally.

Personally, I don't know anyone.

My closest acquaintances are the dirty man with the beard in the next box (we share a common wall) and an elderly black woman who camps under green plastic garbage bags, from time to time, at the end of the alley. I have never spoken to either of them.

Stick 'em #131108 (on the s wall, there are several dozen numbered notes, printed in careful, resolute ballpoint ink) mentions a theory about the verbal origin of certain diseases (shingles, bad smelly farts, fibrodisplasia ossificans and plantar warts) and advises against exchanging words without a physician's certificate. I am not the sort of man to be stampeded by medical gossip. I don't recall having read of this particular pathogenesis anywhere else. But in my study of the numbered stick 'ems, I have found them, on the whole, to be measured, rational and strongly argued.

Therefore, a word to the wise.

My name is It. The woman called me Tom, a clear case of mistaken identity. I find no reference to anyone named Tom on the walls of my box.

Some of the stick 'ems are so old they have fallen down (especially those which hang upon the wall I share with the dirty, bearded man; he brushes against his side of the wall in a most annoying fashion, deliberately, I think sometimes, causing it to bulge inward and shed its burden of yellow papers). I have gathered these up carefully and keep them safe in another box, formerly used to store a pair of size 9½ shoes (I can still smell the fresh, clean leather smell — it makes me feel very rich). I never know when the writer of the words might return to claim his property.

Some of these oldest notes bear the scrawled initials T. W. It could be that Tom, the woman's husband, used to live in my box. Perhaps he even built this fine cardboard home.

This might explain her tearful insistence.

I could not, however, find the words to reveal my thoughts to her. I racked my brains while she stood outside weeping and I crouched inside thinking. But I had forgotten the first thing about communicating with another person.

Did I address her as "my dear madame" or "Hester" or "you fucking pig"?

I wanted to be polite; I wanted to make a good impression. I wanted to open myself right up to her so that she could see she was mistaken and yet not be embarrassed about it. (Often in the streets, I see myself coming along and only realize when we have passed that it was some other person entirely. If a man can have this much trouble simply distinguishing himself from casual passersby, how much more difficult must it be to keep track of someone named Tom?)

In vain, I switched on the penlight attached to my cap to facilitate indoor reading (in the interests of conserving heat, there are no windows in my box; this also has the effect of increasing the amount of useable space for stick 'ems) and perused notes at random, searching for a hint as to the proper mode of address.

Stick 'em #119735, s wall, ll quadrant: *She hath the loyalty of a windsock, the passions of a he-goat and the judgment of a golf tee. I have fixed her wagon though. I have put the darning needle through her diaphragm.*

Stick 'em, unnumbered, ceiling collection, sw quadrant: *The male organ is a thing of wondrous beauty but requires strict attention in matters of hygiene or it will drop off. Other names for male member are my little man and one-eyed trouser snake.*

Ed. Note: It is clear from internal evidence that the wall stick 'ems, taken as a whole, are a composite work. I have identified no less than eighteen distinct authorial styles to which, in interests of future scholarship, I have given the following provisional designations: A, B, C, D, rabbit dick, Leffingwell, Quisenberry, T.W., Ronald, hammer toe, heartsick, Hester, my little man, Arturo Negril Q and W, Edward Note and Z.

It is not obvious from the texts when any of these notes were written or the events described therein occurred. But the numbered stick 'ems clearly relate to a partial concordance on the s wall (ll quadrant) where water seepage has destroyed alphabetized listings from the letter F on. I myself have begun a reconstruction of the missing indices in conjunction with an overall cross-referencing to include unnumbered stick 'ems, boxed stick 'ems and a stack of old issues of the NEW YORK TIMES which I use as a mattress (also a tattered paperback biography of Julio Iglesias, with the last fifty pages missing, which I found in the corner).

Mysteriously, several articles have been clipped from the newspapers and have disappeared. At some point, I intend to visit a library and track down the lost news items so as to include them in my global concordance under a separate heading for non-existent words, words thought and not said, words better left unsaid, forgotten words, words said in haste and regretted, words said too late to do any good, and words said when there is no one to hear them.

My name is It. I know no other.

A woman followed me to my box, claiming to be my wife. She addressed me as Tom, a clear case of mistaken identity. She had red hair.

My closest companions are the dirty, bearded man in the next box and an elderly black woman who camps occasionally under a tent of plastic garbage bags at the end of the alley. I speak to neither of them; we guard our privacy.

The red-haired woman tried to crawl into my box after me, and I was forced to use violence to protect my property.

I blacked her eye for her.

She crawled in after me on all fours, resting her gloved

hands on the foot of my newspaper pallet, and said, "Tommy, we have to talk. I know you're coming around to the apartment at night and ringing the doorbell and running off. Lance followed you in his car. We have to talk."

So I blacked her eye for her.

Boo-hoo.

I was nearly undone by the gross intimacy of it all, the closeness of the red-haired woman, with her bosoms hanging down, her rump in the air (I could, of course, only imagine this), the smell of her pomatum mixing with the foetid, cardboardy smell of my box, and the casual and familiar way she referred to Lance.

She backed out with a kid glove over her eye, whimpering.

*Hester*, I thought, in a fugitive sort of way, not knowing of whom I cogitated.

She sat splay-legged against the front of my box, with her feet standing up at right angles to the damp pavement, nursing her eye and sobbing. Her back made the inside ul and ll quadrants (e wall) buckle alarmingly (the ur and lr quadrants had been cut away to facilitate ingress and egress, i.e. the door). A half-dozen stick 'ems dropped off, making a papery clisp-clisp sound as they fell.

I was overwrought and upset at the intrusion (Stick 'em LOAT #81: *A man's box is his castle.*) and the outrageousness of her insane accusations, not to mention the implication that unseen spies were shadowing me to my very doorstep and the horrifying thought that total strangers might have free access to the premises in my absence.

The dirty, bearded man coughed in the next box, a kind of sniggering cough, a cough that screamed collusion with my enemies.

*Hester*, I thought again, uncontrollably.

*Her breasts, I'll have to move*, I thought.

I have begun renumbering the numbered stick 'ems using a system of my own devising, prefixed by the letters LOAT, an acronym for the phrase List Of All Things. Hence, for example, Stick 'em #131108, under the new system, becomes Stick 'em LOAT #92.

The LOAT system itself raises a host of philosophical and grammatical — not to mention medical, lexicographical, numerological and gnostic — questions, questions which I intend to deal with in a separate preface to the LOAT Concordance.

To name only one:

1) What is the relationship of the LOAT numbers to the original numbers? Take, for example, the stick 'em in reference, LOAT #92 (a brief, yet scholarly disquisition on the theory of word-borne disease vectors), formerly designated as Stick 'em #131108.

Divide 92 by 131108 and you get .000701. Multiply them and you get 12,061,936. Are these results simply random arithmetical products or do they refer in some obscure way to other, lost or as yet unnumbered, stick 'ems?

Do the walls of my box conceal a hidden pattern discoverable only on mathematical grounds?

2) Why have I been able to trace and renumber only three hundred and eighty-seven numbered stick 'ems, when my predecessor or predecessors were able to number them in the hundreds of thousands? Does this mean a vast trove of painstakingly inscribed notations has simply disappeared?

It has occurred to me that the dirty, bearded man and the elderly black woman, with her sinister green garbage bags, are not above suspicion in this regard. It could be that they have entered my box on occasions when I have been out foraging for food and deliberately stolen or rearranged my stick 'ems in order to torment me.

Thinking about this possibility often drives me to despair. Someone meddling with my stick 'ems, even the slightest pencilled alteration to a text, would render all my efforts otiose. The text must be pristine and untouched for me to be able to read the correct meanings into it.

The uncertainty caused by thoughts of lost or stolen stick 'ems or false entries (of comic or sadistic origin) causes me to alternate between profound fatalism and extreme paranoia (see relevant psychological notes — s wall, both u quadrants).

The red-haired woman went away, but I was a shaking wreck.

Her sobs and the texture of her sturdy brow and cheek bones against the knuckles of my hand had left me completely undone and exhausted.

A fragmentary thought crossed my mind — *Depleted by passion* . . .

Then I realized the words were a phrase on Stick 'em LOAT #153, sw quadrant, ceiling collection (I noted with satisfaction how easy it was to use the new system) which read: *Depleted by passion, the successful lover withdraws into himself after coitus in order to recuperate the energies discharged into the amourous and unassuageable female. The cycle repeats itself, though each time he becomes weaker. His very success creates in her the desire, the lack, the absence, into which he, driven by instinct, throws himself again and again until released from this onerous duty by Death. The female is apparently able to have multiple organisms without any ill effect whatsoever.*

There were several LOAT cross-references, this being a key text, alarming in its implications, including a reference to LOAT #1107, a little etymological essay which I had written myself on that troubling word "organisms."

I felt better after reading this and spent the remainder

of the day supine on my *NEW YORK TIMES* mattress, staring at the stick 'ems above my face. After a time, the penlight on my hat went out and I was in the dark. It was better thus. In the dark, I could brush my fingers ever so lightly across the stick 'ems as if they were a woman's nape hairs I happened to be caressing.

In the morning, when I awoke, I discovered that several ceiling stick 'ems had fallen on me in the night, dry and quiet as autumn leaves. I urinated in an old milk carton and spent a happy hour with my glue pot re-sticking the stick 'ems in their proper places.

Ed. Note: Here follow several unnumbered stick 'ems to be cross-referenced using the key word "morning."

Mornings, now that it is cold, the dirty, bearded man and I rise late and sit at the doors of our respective dwellings, stuffing old newspapers under our clothes for added insulation. Wordlessly, we pass individual sections back and forth. He is a shallow fellow, dressing himself in the *POST* or the sports and business sections of better papers, to the exclusion of all else. I myself love the feel of the *TIMES BOOK REVIEW* and the Tuesday *SCIENCE TIMES* next to my skin.

The ink rubs off, leaving snippets of articles and headlines on my chest, back and thighs. When I go to the mission for my monthly shower, I often enjoy reviewing past events in the mirror, before getting under the water. The chance juxtapositions and inter-cuttings make a kind of found poetry that is often delightfully witty.

Of course, there were other men at the mission who use newspapers for underwear. The dressing room is the next best thing to a library reading room. Certain lower class types sport huge headline smears from the tabloids. Oth-

ers bear smudged, yet incisive, economic analyses from the
WALL STREET JOURNAL.

I am the only real reader in the group. Sometimes this
has led to misunderstandings and embarrassments.


The woman who claimed to be my wife has red hair. She returned this morning and spoke briefly with my neighbour,
an act which filled me with foreboding.

I was unable to continue my work and had to go out.

In the street, I encountered several well-meaning indi-
viduals who pressed money on me (though I make a good
living carrying a sandwich board around Times Square
three evenings a week; I am a human sign which reads:
GIRLS, GIRLS, GIRLS! LIVE SEX ACTS! HE-SHES! GREEK AND FRENCH TRANSLATIONS! NO COVER!
FREE HOTDOGS AT MIDNIGHT!).

I went to the mission for my monthly shower though it
had only been four days since my last. The concierge re-
marked upon this, a liberty and invasion of privacy to
which I could not respond because of the angry feelings
which welled up inside me. He told me to stop reading
other people in the shower as this annoyed them.

In spite of the concierge's injunction, I read parts of
several informative TIMES pieces while I soaked under a
thin stream of lukewarm water. One article dealt with the
mysterious disappearance of Pancho Villa's head, another
discoursed on the End of History, an event, apparently,
which occurred only a few short weeks ago.

When I returned to my box, the dirty, bearded man was
pacing up and down before my door in an agitated manner. As soon as he sighted me, he came running over,
shouting, "There was a woman here to see you. She talked
to me. I think she wanted sex. I've always had an effect on
women. That's how I ended up here. My health cracked."

I didn't know what to say. He seemed so excited, so very

pleased with himself *her breasts and red hair,* giving me his whole history and health record like that. I couldn't just turn away from him.

So we sat a while with our backs to the alley wall, watching the elderly black woman rummage in a dumpster. This was a profound moment of communion, let me tell you, though it ended abruptly when I tried to share my thoughts on the LOAT Concordance with him. The dirty, bearded man said something rude, and we ended up wrestling and spitting in one another's face.

The elderly black woman screamed at us, "Aaaooorrw! Aaaooorrw!" She seemed to derive some evil pleasure from our conflict.

(Aged stick 'em, shoebox collection: *The most common human experience is betrayal. All our relations are contaminated with sadness and terror.* [Ed. Note: A depressing thought.])


3) Then there is the infinity problem.

I am composing the LOAT Concordance and its explanatory preface on fresh unnumbered stick 'ems (there is a large supply in another corner of my box, origin unknown) which I glue to the ceiling in orderly rows easily readable from a recumbent position (sometimes jokingly referred to as "the missionary position") with the aid of my penlight.

I intend to begin numbering the ceiling stick 'ems sequentially as soon as I finish numbering all the previously numbered and unnumbered stick 'ems and the NEW YORK TIMES, also the trademarks, logos, company slogans and shipping instructions on the cardboard walls of my box (some of the box panels face inward, some outward, thus creating horrendous cataloguing problems).

Each numbered stick 'em generates at least two concordance stick 'ems and an abstract to which I append some brief, preliminary conclusions, a tally of possible connections (semantic, spatial or mathematical) with other texts, and assorted stray thoughts. To achieve my goal of total list integration (LOAT), I shall have to include the new concordance stick 'ems as a special subset of all stick 'ems. This means that the set of all stick 'ems grows at the same rate as my system list, making the job of including all stick 'ems within the list impossible to complete.

A task which I once undertook with a light heart, thinking perhaps to while away a few idle hours putting in order the thoughts, observations, quotations, theories, apophthegms, limericks, hypotheses, phone numbers and laundry lists earlier tenants had affixed to my cardboard walls, has turned into a pointless burden.

I worked on reconstructing the water-damaged notes on the s wall. When the red-haired woman knocked at my door, I had finished eighteen LOAT references, a good morning's work.

"Tom?" she inquired, softly and wearily.

She had a black eye, a stunning instance of the convergence of text and reality.

"Tom?"

She was clearly deranged. I was not Tom, though I felt myself beginning to acquire a veneer of Tom-ness through repetition and association. (Ed. Note: See LOAT #437, Arturo Negril Q, s wall, ur quadrant: *The lover attempts to reflect the image of himself which he sees in her eyes. He steps outside of himself and becomes an other, a stranger. This stranger then has an affair with the poor fellow's girlfriend. Ha!* See under Lovers, Paranoid Schizophrenia, Betrayal, L-words, Doubles, Out-of-Body Experiences and Impossible Things.)

Who was Tom? Who was the red-haired woman, for that matter? And the ineffable Lance? (Ed. Note: See under

Love Triangles, Real and Imaginary.) I found myself adrift in a phantasmagoria of things which did not exist: missing NEW YORK TIMES articles, Pancho Villa's head (stolen from his grave in 1926), Tom, words left unsaid, not to mention the numbered stick 'ems which I had failed to locate.

I started to weep, abruptly aware of the futility and hubris compassed by my life in a box.

The red-haired woman seemed to understand. She placed a gloved hand on my ankle and pressed it. Her hair was heavily lacquered. She was wearing trousers and a short jacket made from animal skins. The odour of her perfume — Mankiller — was everywhere.

She was clearly ablaze inside, whether I was Tom or not. I tried to resist, but she was too strong for me, and soon we were involved in an embrace.

To the casual observer, there was little difference between our embrace and the wrestling match I had recently had with the dirty, bearded man.

We knocked over the urine carton.

I caught sight of Stick 'em LOAT #57: *His life was haunted by a sexual sadness.* This made no sense to me whatever.

"Stop it! Stop it, Tommy," she said. "I'm with Lance now. You have to stop living in the past. It's not right what you're doing, making a public spectacle of yourself, hurting your Mom and Pop, harassing Lance and me. Dr. Reinhardt wants you to come back."

Ha, I thought. I knew I was living in a box and that the TIMES had reported the End of History several weeks before. But her beauty gave me pause. I felt sorry for Tom, clearly a man like any other, like myself perhaps, a scholar equally obsessed by his work and this red-haired Siren, a tragic figure.

Her black eye, partially concealed with cream and powder (the smell of which reminded me of my mother), was exceedingly attractive.

I wanted to speak, though when I opened my mouth, I had nothing to say. I felt the need to come to an understanding, for some sort of communication to take place, but the words to express this failed me. From the first onslaught of passion, I had felt my desire begin to wane. I had begun to think of the stick 'ems, ponder the meaning of the relationships, so far undiscovered, between the various authors. The truth was I felt my body dissolve as soon as she touched me. It became evanescent and airy, a thing of dentals and labials; I became nothing but words, ambiguous, ironic, fleeting and slippery.

The moment she touched me I was gone.

She knew this. I could see it by the tears in her eyes.


A new stick 'em has appeared. Blue. A different colour from all the rest. Provenance unknown. I should resolve to stay in my box continuously, but nature drives me out, not to mention the constant hacking and snuffling of the dirty, bearded man next door, his amorous sighs — my mind boggles at what is going on in the next box.

Blue Stick 'em LOAT #492 (it was such an event, finding a new stick 'em, that I registered it immediately in the List Of All Things): *Dr. Elkho Reinhardt, 3:30 p.m., Thursday. H.*

I think the dirty, bearded man and the elderly black woman have formed a liaison, a cabal, a plot, against me. Alternatively, it has occurred to me that the dirty, bearded man and I are identical (he bears the marks and scars of It-ness), or that he is the author of at least some of the stick 'em entries, the ones exhibiting a peculiar sexual obsessiveness, for example LOAT #12: *She hath an organ that smells like a wet horse blanket; by the size of it, I warrant she hath been entertaining large herbivores; she pisseth continuously, noisily and in huge volume. The house is awash!* (Ed. Note: See under LOAT #92.)

I took off my clothes to examine myself. On my shrunken member, I found the words: *Several women in the chamber broke into sobs. Some men buried their faces in their hands.* Under my left nipple, I read: *Wandlitz, the name of the elite compound outside East Berlin, soon became a synonym for corruption.* And using a hand mirror, I discovered, imprinted on my buttocks, the words: *The most serious allegations for now are those against Mr. Schalck-Golodkowsky, but his dealings could not compete for public indignation with the revelations of the lifestyle of the elite.*

I made appropriate notes and stuck them to the common wall.

I was extremely pleased. Clues were beginning to point to this man Schalck-Golodkowsky as the agent of all my distress. I barely thought of the red-haired woman *her breasts* until I perceived that she was walking up and down outside my box, slapping her hands against her sides to keep warm, her breath going up like smoke.

How long had she been there?

I felt a sudden thrill of fear. Having decided at the outset to eliminate the time element from the LOAT Concordance and Preface on sound philosophical grounds (the number and contents of the original stick 'ems being fixed, time references were assumed superfluous), I now found myself with no objective scale for determining the sequence of events referred to on the walls of my box.

How many times had she visited? The words "morning" and "Thursday" suddenly appeared less fixed and precise than hitherto assumed. The morning of what day? I thought, *Hester I am all alone and you with your toy man.* Or were they all the same morning? The urine carton was full again, so one could deduce that time had passed since it was overturned. But how much time? How long had I been there? Where did I come from?

The red-haired woman had cast me out of the Eden of

my certainties and flung me into the Hell of relativity. (LOAT #87: *Her nether hair hangeth even to her knees.*)

When I poked my head out of my box, she said, "It's Thursday. You're late. You were out at the store yesterday, bothering Lance's customers. I've come to take you."

I threw the milk carton full of urine over her and walked to the door of the box occupied by the dirty, bearded man. In the murky darkness of his dwelling, I could see him and the elderly black woman with their ears pressed against the common wall.

I have you now, Mr. Schalck-Golodkowsky, I thought in triumph.

Clicking my heels with aristocratic disdain, I gave them a curt nod and said, "*Guten abend.*"


I went to the mission for my monthly shower. The concierge mentioned quite rudely that I had only been there the day before. I went into the common shower and immediately noticed, on a fellow bather's shoulder-blade, the words I had so recently (?) recorded: *Several women in the chamber broke into sobs. Some men buried their faces in their hands.*

The concierge ushered me into the street once more, begging me never to return. Apparently, I had been following the words with my fingertip, my devil's finger.

I felt the same painful embarrassment a boy feels when caught touching his member by his Mom. I want my Hester, I thought, in a bleak and fleeting sort of way. What was a Hester?

I thought of going to the library to check on this, but went by the alley which I now believed was called Wandlitz, a place of vice and corruption. Old Schalck-Golodkowsky invited me to share a bottle of Thunderbird with him and the elderly black woman. They had the sign of venery over their door, but I could not refuse their kind offer. I wiped the mouth of the bottle with a dirty sock before taking a sip.

"Yer missus were har win you wuz out," said Frau Schalck-Golodkowsky. For the first time, I noticed she had only one eye. She was very old, upwards of one hundred and fifty, I should have guessed, looking into that morbid orb. Her words struck me as having a persecutory ring.

She broke wind alarmingly. Old Schalck-Golodkowsky giggled.

What did it all mean? I asked myself — the red-haired woman and the sudden unreliability of words; Tom and his evil twin, Lance; their collusion with the dirty, bearded man and the elderly black woman, now unmasked as the nefarious Schalck-Golodkowskys; the fresh note of asperity in the voice of the mission concierge; and the messages on the walls of my box, which had once seemed so open and eloquent, so ready to give up their meaning, offer advice, make predictions about past events, which, until so recently (?), had seemed about to body forth for me their laws, structures and universal explanations in simple lists, diagrams and equations?

I had wanted to thank the old couple for the wine, but words failed me.

In fact, I began to suspect I was suffering from some sort of speech impediment — fibrodisplasia ossificans progressiva of the vocal line-out. I had become the words on my walls, but had lost my voice. It was a strange condition, let me tell you (though I won't, or I wouldn't, except for the large number of fresh stick 'ems which allow me to make notes on the progress of my disease *her heart beneath her breasts, Hester* and leave them here upon the wall — LOAT #401 et passim — for later scholars of boxology, psychoarchaeologists and linguists of all persuasions; make no mistake, I am on the cutting edge of *a nervous breakdown* research into the limits of dis*(inter)*course, the pathology of s*(ex)*peech acts, the drag net of language, which floats through the sea of life killing everything that comes to it).

The wine had made me paranoid.

After an immense effort, I found a library.

I was able to trace one of the missing NEW YORK TIMES articles, a report on new developments in cosmology. Indications are that the universe would not have turned out the way it has unless there existed huge amounts of matter as yet unnoticed and unaccounted for. This missing stuff, the source of mysterious and powerful gravitational forces which shape our destinies, is called dark matter.

I knew at once that the red-haired woman and her minions, the synecdochic Lance and the S-Gs, were at the bottom of this. It wouldn't have surprised me to discover that the S-Gs had been secreting vast amounts of dark matter in that box next door to mine (suspicious coughs, amorous noises, cries of joy).

I left the library vindicated and went over to the mission for a shower, but was not allowed inside.


Stick 'em, unnumbered, shoe box collection: *The messages from the past rustle on the walls of my little home when the wind blows or when the dirty, bearded man brushes against the wall. I feel a kinship with the mysterious, lost writers, the ancient ones who penned their thoughts and stuck them inside the box — strange cardboard bottle floating on the concrete sea-pavements of the city.* (Ed. Note: The concluding sentences are in red ink and written by a different hand.) *The ancient anatomists were wiser than they knew when they chose to call the exterior female organ "labia" — lips as in mouth and as in the phonetic designation labial — thus etymologically linking the power of speech with a woman's nether parts (which, I have heard it said, are capable of generating sound and rudimentary speech acts by the sucking in and sudden expulsion of air). The noble male member, by contrast, is mute, stoic and incapable of falseness. It is the source of univocal meaning. When a woman speaketh, so says the Sumerian prophet Raz-el-dorab, it is prudent to stand up-wind.*

The trick is to read all individual texts as part of one vast narrative the meaning of which will become clear as we approach textual totality (TT), that is when we have arranged enough or all of the individual texts (textuals or textettes) — the jig-saw puzzle analogy is helpful here — in their proper order.

At TT, for example, it will be possible, at last, to decide if life (L) is meant to be read as a comedy or a tragedy, as romance or thriller, or some combination of genres, styles and points of view.

It will also be possible to arrive at some *endlich* theoretical conclusions as to the nature of AOAT (the Author Of All Things, God, Amenhotep, Tom Wyatt, Herr S-G, or whatever name it will be proved He goes by — all clues pointing to the writer being blessed with possession of a one-eyed trouser snake [Ed. Note: Except for the blue stick 'ems!]).

Of course, it must be admitted at the outset that TT, L and AOAT are all hypothetical constructs, moot, unproven and highly speculative. The LOAT Concordance and Preface are meant to be a sort of prolegomena, a kind of ground-clearing exercise and first attempt at TT, a preliminary structuring, if you will, of the hard data.

I returned to Wandlitz in haste, eager to put to paper my most recent impressions. It seemed to me, all things being equal, that TT = (t)n, where t stands for any individual textette and n is *Hester's bra size* the number of all existing, possible, putative, potential, virtual, spurious, forged, false and inspired textettes (or textuals [Ed. Note:

It seems that the use of the technical terms "textette" and "textual" formed the basis of a heated scholarly debate among the authors represented inside the box. Half seem to follow Arturo Negril W in preferring the feminized "textette," while the other half swear by rabbit dick who coined the designation "textual." There is even some internal evidence to the effect that C and Ronald were living in the box at the same time as rabbit dick and that the latter was forced to leave after promulgating his heretical jargon.])

The following equation then describes, in a form at once succinct, perspicuous and elegant — after all, scientific criteria are ultimately aesthetic — the meaning of existence: $(t)n/AOAT = L$.

I was tremendously excited by this discovery and only slightly worried about thoughts of dark matter, words left unsaid, Pancho Villa's head and the mysterious blue stick 'ems. I resolved not to spare myself in my efforts to complete the LOAT Concordance, but as I turned the corner into the alley (Wandlitz, East German Sodom, Box City) I was nearly run down by a bright-yellow city sanitation truck.

The elderly black woman (a.k.a. Frau Schalck-Golodkowsky, the Whore of Babylon, paramour of my neighbour, dark twin star of the red-haired woman *Hester* — in a flash, terrible doubts assailed me; what if L = Labia, Lance, or Lovelorn? Alliteration was only a circumstantial clue, yet no scientific or scholarly mind could ignore it; only a painstaking series of experiments could settle the issue) sat weeping in the doorway of Herr S-G's box, wiping her tears and blowing her nose in a green plastic garbage bag.

She said, "'e was takin' a shit in da dumpter an' det took oom away!"

I was struck speechless. (Ed. Note: Progressive fibrodisplasia ossificans was first diagnosed by the French physician Guy Patin in 1692. In the course of the disease, muscle turns to cartilage and then calcifies. As the tongue is a muscle, speechlessness is often the first symptom of onset. The patient generally dies after a few years by shattering, either from being dropped on the floor by clumsy attendants or by being knocked accidentally against door jambs. This is, of course, the origin of the term "brokenhearted.")

As you know, I had never trusted these people. I could tell they held some mean-spirited grudge against me, perhaps through nothing more than sheer envy at my superior ambition and intellect ("Snob!" he would hiss every time I stuffed a fresh BOOK REVIEW down the back of my pants). Sometimes, however, I suspected them of more facinorous motivations, suspected, yes, that they were in league with (dupes, paid informants, hit men) unseen forces (dark matter, Hester, the Toys R Us corporation) out to compass my ruin — on the whole things had been going badly for me, oh, for the last thirty or forty years.

Still, it was a shock. We all used the dumpster as a comfort station, careless of the dangers involved. I thought of old S-G, neighbour, drinking companion, fellow cardboard troglodyte, honourable opponent, cut off and swept away in the act of defecation.

*Sic transit gloria mundi*, I said to myself.

My heart went out to the sad, old woman in her hour of sorrow. I wanted to say something comforting, but words failed me. (Ed. Note: As usual. See *supra*.)

I reached out a hand and touched her trembling shoulder.

This is what life is like, I thought, loved ones disappearing for no reason, when your back was turned, going off in city sanitation trucks or with fast-talking toy entrepreneurs

from New Jersey, leaving you bereft, empty and wordless.
What could it all mean?

At this moment, the red-haired woman drove up in a
car with New York licence plates (I had thought, from internal evidence, that we were living in East Berlin), a
dozen or so new blue stick 'ems in full view on the dash.
She was wearing a plastic raincoat with the hood up.

I started off to the mission for my monthly shower,
when she screamed "Stop!"

She went over to the elderly black woman and asked
her what was wrong.

Frau S-G repeated her obscure but heart-rending story.
I really wanted a shower, having, in the red-haired
woman's presence, a strong desire to scrub my little man.
But I could find no words to express my desires.

What I had begun to notice was that I had times when
my energy was up, when all things seemed possible, when I
would throw myself into my work with a positive and opti-
mistic attitude; while at other times I was confused, fearful,
melancholic, assailed by doubts, uninterested in even the
simplest words. (What if, I suddenly thought, L = Lami-
nate, Lobworm or Laxative?. Once the argument for
alliteration was admitted, all sorts of horrific and Lunatic
possibilities became thinkable.)

I felt the latter most strongly, as I say, in the presence of
the red-haired woman, who at that moment was busy trying to squeeze Mme S-G into the back seat of her car.

I craned my neck and tried to read one of the blue stick
'ems — LOAT #92. With a growing sense of alarm, I realized she had fathomed my system, had tumbled to the
LOAT Concordance and had begun fabricating false
(though blue) entries to the List Of All Things *en masse.*
This filled me with dread.

The red-haired woman had subdued Mrs. S-G who was

blubbering in the back; I found myself in the front passenger seat of a BMW sedan (proof, I thought, of the German connection) with a Blaupunkt tapedeck blaring my favourite Julio Iglesias tape. We sped off at once, leaving the Sink of Sin, Wandlitz, in pursuit of the yellow city sanitation truck.

Though I still had nothing to say, I admired the red-haired woman for her decisiveness, her quick-witted willingness to intercede on behalf of old Schalck-Golodkowsky and his stricken lover. My own obsession with words, with the LOAT Concordance, with *her breasts*, subterranean plots, infidelities, ambiguities, showers, stick 'ems, concierges, etc., rendered me useless in a situation that called for action. At the same time, I really despised her for foisting her vision of reality on me, for her constant references to Tom, her persistence (the black eye had all but healed), and the truly insidious scheme to introduce spurious stick 'ems (blue) into the box at Wandlitz.

I caught a glimpse of my face in the side mirror. On my cheek I could clearly make out the words: *Several women in the chamber broke into sobs. Some men buried their faces in their hands.* I carefully laid a hand over my cheek so as to preserve the message till I had a chance to transfer it to a stick 'em.

The sanitation truck came into view just ahead of us. Old Schalck-G was in the process of climbing out the back, though his progress was impeded by the circumstance of his pants being down around his ankles and also somehow caught in the machinery.

With my free hand, I rifled through the stack of blue stick 'ems on the dash. Out of the corner of my eye, I noticed the red-haired woman glance at me as she threaded the grid-locked traffic. (It was a strange city; sometimes it seemed to me that cars stood motionless at blocked intersections for years on end, their bodies dissolving into piles of rust, mice making homes in their engines, their drivers growing old at the wheel.)

Horns were blaring.

Frau S-G was screaming, "Aaaoorw! Aaaoorw!"

Blue LOAT #1287: *We all love you and pray for you but Lance is about to call the police. He says somebody tried to jimmy the back door of the store.*

Blue LOAT #37: *You wrote all those stick 'ems yourself. H.*

My mind was in a state of ultra-confusion.

The dirty, bearded man fell off the sanitation truck into the path of a Yellow Cab. A Haitian cabbie jumped out and began to shout French epithets.

I recalled LOAT #37 in the box (yes, in her haste, she had duplicated an already extant stick 'em number): *Man hath an eye for eternity; his works are multifarious, austere and transcendent; his Organ is the Rod of Justice. Woman hath a wayward eye; her purpose on Earth is obscure; she is a Temptress, and her Organ is the Swamp of Iniquity.* (Ed. Note: Once again the hand-writing changes in mid-text.) *She says she loves me, but she just woke up one morning and knew she would die if she didn't change her life. She says I don't listen to her, that I make funny whistling sounds with my nose when I sleep, that I gobble my food in barbaric and gluttonous haste (watching me eat makes her want to be sick), that I bore her with my constant complaints against Fate and mediocre people ("Look who's talking," she says). She hates Julio Iglesias and the* NEW YORK TIMES *and thinks my nervous laugh is maniacal.* (Ed. Note: Not exactly what one would call a ringing indictment.) *Evidently, changing her life means going out with L., who once gave her a t-shirt with the motto "Life's A Beach" printed on it. How can she take seriously a man who has made a career in Barbie dolls?*

We passed the mission, which was only three doors along from where Mr. S-G lay in the street. I tried to get out, but a Yellow Cab prevented me from opening my door.

"Why don't you say something?" asked the red-haired woman (pretty, eyes the colour of blue stick 'ems; only my dedication to the LOAT Concordance and a certain ratine — of or relating to the genus rat — toy drummer stood between us). Hester's name *her breasts, her heart, her dear heart* were on the tip of my tongue, but the curse of silence was upon me. (Ed. Note: *Supra.*) Speech — evanescent, hasty, unconsidered, polysemous — evaded me; far more did I trust the written word which had a tendency to stay put (unlike women, *viz.* Stick 'em #128777: *A woman's words are as substantial as a ferret's fart. Trust them not.*) — grapheme over phoneme, those were my watchwords.

I wanted to get back to my box, to lose myself in my work, to drug myself with the infinite and loving analysis of the notes, signs and commercial heiroglyphs which festooned the walls of my corrugated home.

(We had, by this time, crawled through the car windows and retrieved the dirty, bearded man — a.k.a. you-know-who — much soiled by his recent proximity to the interior of the city sanitation truck. We helped him pull up what was left of his pants — all sorts of surprising and interesting reading material falling out of his clothes as we did so: several issues of the GUARDIAN, a December 12, 1989, PRAVDA, sports pages from RUDE PRAVO and the FRANK-FURTER ZEITUNG, and five identical copies of the PARTISAN REVIEW dating from the spring of 1984. This sanitation truck incident had revealed new qualities to me; already I liked him better. Several of the stick 'ems, I was certain, had been written in a little known Croatian dialect. Now I felt sure the dirty, bearded man was just the person to help me decipher them.)

Ed. Note: I had a dream last night. I dreamt that the elderly black woman wasn't: a) elderly, or b) black. We were making love in the box next door, this Cyclopean woman and I. She was about twenty, with one eye like a green grape and the other normal. Her lustrous red hair seemed to wreath her head in flames. As time passed, I became aware that the blackness of her skin had nothing to do with her pigmentation. She was covered from head to foot with a tattoo. Upon closer inspection, the tattoo resolved itself into incredibly tiny letters, words, sentences, paragraphs and chapters. I took out my magnifying glass — having lost interest entirely in our love-making — and began to read her body. I read and read. It seemed as though it would take a million years to read the whole book. I was only down to her left nipple (an amazing spiral nebula of a tone poem made up of concentrated miniaturized letters totalling upwards of one hundred thousand words) when I woke up. I could remember nothing of what I'd read, except that it was wonderful, better than the best sex. When I woke up, I felt as if everything was going to be all right, as if, finally, I would be happy again. I thought, She is the Mother of the World.


**2**


It did not fulfil his goal of translating the Croatian stick 'ems with Prof. Schalck-Golodkowsky's help. Old S-G returned to Wandlitz, but he had clearly lost heart after his accidental run-in with the city sanitation truck.

Constipation was perhaps his main problem.

His wife, growing less and less articulate, began to beat him mercilessly with old shoe boxes.

Eventually, he abandoned his surface home altogether, went to live in the subway and was heard from no more.

He had tears in his eyes and stopped to give It a fond little wave of farewell as he staggered out of the alley the last time.

The elderly black woman pined for him (this is one of the mysteries of human existence: how a woman can hate a man, beat him mercilessly with shoe boxes and then dwindle as though she had a tape worm when he is gone). She and It had a brief, frenzied and melancholy affair, a relationship they both regretted later.

It probably summed it up best when he wrote in LOAT #2073: *We were both lonely, sad creatures. We had both suffered grievously in life, had both felt love and been abandoned. It was natural that, without thinking much, we should lurch toward one another in the hour of our need. But she was not a reader, and we both soon realized there could be no lasting attachment.*

Eventually, the elderly black woman left Wandlitz, too, heading, she said, for El Cajon, a San Diego suburb where she believed she might have family.

The neighbouring box fell into decay, and It had to take special measures to ensure the structural integrity of the common wall.

But Wandlitz had lost its Weimar Republic charm for him. The fruitful period, when moral decadence strode hand-in-hand with intense intellectual activity (like Nero fiddling while Paramus burned), had given way to an era of stagnation, cultural anomie and mounting anti-Semitism.

In this atmosphere of malaise, It quit his job as a human sign and began to take money from the red-haired woman and her toy mogul boyfriend on the condition that he make twice-weekly visits to Dr. Elkho Reinhardt, a prominent Upper West Side analyst. For a month that spring, It sank so low as to impersonate Tom Wyatt, the red-haired woman's former husband, in order to encourage the doctor and extort additional funds from the guilty (if deranged) couple.

This time of drift came abruptly to an end one afternoon when It (who never lost his native fastidiousness) adjourned to the mission for his monthly shower. There, for all to see, wrapped around the broad buttocks of a fellow mission client in sixty-point type, was a NEW YORK POST headline: PARAMUS TOY STORE FIRE BOMBED/ MANAGER DESCRIBES BARBIE DOLL "HOLOCAUST."

He knew at once this was the proverbial writing on the wall, though how he knew he could not tell. Only, the sudden and mysterious linkage of the words "Paramus," "toy store," "fire" and "manager" — words which had hitherto appeared exclusively within the confines of his box — struck him as evidence of a disturbing synchronicity, a gathering of *her breasts* forces (Lance, dark matter) bent on his destruction.

Alarmed, yet lucid, realizing he must somehow save himself, he went underground within hours — first sealing his box with duct tape and mailing it to himself under an assumed named (Leffingwell), c/o General Delivery, El Paso, Texas.

Such practical action on It's part may surprise the casual reader. But he had always possessed a special affinity for the phrase "parcel post," and the sight of a Federal Express truck parked in the street beyond the alley never failed to inspire in him the frisson of adventurous anticipation other people feel at airports and train stations.

(Also, he had eaten a Mexican orange that morning, which he regarded as a sign. From his investigation into the disappearance of Pancho Villa's head, he knew El Paso was on the way to Mexico.)

It took two weeks to make his way across the country, travelling at night on Greyhound buses, using money he had saved from his therapy job for food and tickets.

In El Paso, he collected his box, then slipped across the border in the back of a crowded cattle truck.

Changing his name yet again (A. Negril), he journeyed south to the village of Ococingo near the Guatemalan border, where he now resides in a small, rented room above a brothel that goes by the name of a large American battery manufacturer. He earns his living as a letter-writer among the credulous and illiterate Chiapan peasants, while continuing his boxological research.

It is neither happy nor sad.

The passions of his youth are spent. He has to wear eyeglasses to read and make notes.

The brothel denizens regard him as a harmless and amusing eccentric and delight in spending a restful hour or two sitting in his box (it just fits inside the rented room, with space to spare for a hotplate and icebox), listening to Julio Iglesias tapes and sipping iced tea while the old man scribbles on his little yellow pads.

Sleeping, he dreams tropical dreams, full of talkative parrots and red-haired women.

And if, by chance, some distant night sound disturbs him and he wakes, It will step out on his tiny balcony, wipe his glasses and peer upward, marvelling at the innumerable pinpricks of light which spangle the firmament. At such moments, he feels the deepest peace. For in his heart, he knows that what he sees is nothing but the ceiling of yet another vast and mysterious box.

Edward Note

Calle Borracho
Ococingo, Chiapas

# A GUIDE TO ANIMAL BEHAVIOUR

I am in bed with a woman who looks like a movie star, and I have lost my memory.

The movie star woman is asleep, which is lucky and gives me a chance to try to remember who I am and how I got here. She is evidently a person of low virtue. I can see she is shamelessly naked, as I am myself, I might add. And she is snoring. I find the combination of her beauty, her shamelessness and her snores moving in strange and delightful ways.

When she wakes up, she is almost as suspicious of me as I of her, though she has the advantage of knowing who she is.

"How did this happen?" I say.

"You were cute," she says. "When I asked you your name, you looked at your watch and said, 'Seiko Quartz.'"

Her name is Tracy Mondesire — used to be Tracy Gittles from Boogie Ridge, Levy County (the only county in the U.S.A. named for a Jewish person), Florida. Her family were Flat-Out Baptists, but died young, and she was brought up by Grammy and Grampy Gittles in a car-part heaven outside Ocala.

Grammy and Grampy Gittles were fat and blind and stood four square for the Bible and segregation. Grampy Gittles swore he'd die before they had a "coloured" TV in the house. He wrote verses for the local paper and communed with the dead with the aid of a hollow cow horn.

Several strange men interfered with her while she was growing up, but it was nothing she minded.

Glitter is the only life she ever wanted.

They tell me we are living in Bel Air. Does Washington know about this place?

Our swimming pool has an undertow.

I have set off the burglar alarm eighty-two times since moving in.

She sells real estate to Arabs, nothing under a mil and a half.

She can suck air into her hole and blow pussy farts. It is the damnedest thing to see.

She reads pornographic books to raise her spirits and sometimes will sit home of an evening with a stack of filthy cassettes as high as your elbow. I am not much for seeing it on the screen myself.

Wherever you go in this house, there is odour of muff.

One morning, I tackle Juanita, the maid, out of pure aggression. Evidently, Juanita has had her eye on me as well. We do it in a chair until there is nothing left of me but a little pool of sweat. I wake up on the living room floor, with Tracy trying to get my thing between the blades of the garden shears.

She fires Juanita without notice, then hires her back a week later because she cannot bear to be cruel to anyone who makes less than two hundred thousand a year.

After a year or so, we get married. It is a clamouring and tasteless affair with eight hundred guests and house ads in the toilets.

"Eat me," she says, lying on the bed with her legs in the air. This is an inviting subject for the Old Masters, let me tell you. I am not certain it is the manly thing to do, but I love to mumble her pussy, and it drives her wild.

I read in the *ENQUIRER* that I once flew DC-3s up from Colombia, but turned for the state after crash-landing three tons of high-grade in a peanut field surrounded by federal agents. I fingered Richard Estramadura, arch-international crime kingpin, before he went into hiding. He has taken out a million-dollar contract on my life. I ask Tracy is this is true. "He made it up," she says, pointing to Don, her publicist. I do not know if I should be upset that this over-sedated weeny is inventing my life.

To keep in shape, I do daily workouts with an S & W .357. Nights, I do speed and sneak up on coyotes in the backyard.

I drive a pink Fleetwood with zebra-skin seatcovers and an oog-gah horn. She gave it to me for my birthday. How do I know when my birthday is? I don't. But she says I must have had one some time.

Ten years have passed. I have learned to walk sideways in the street to cut down wind resistance. I have only strayed five or six times, that Tracy knows about.

I don't know how this happened, but we are having one hell of a time together.

A woman stopped me in the street the other day. I was wearing aviator shades, eight gold chains, a button that said "Drugs Saved My Life" and expensive white shoes made by poor people in Brazil. She said she was my wife. She said she had married my brother Daken after I left like that. She and Daken had just flown in from Kentucky to be on "Wheel of Fortune." We have three children, all brought up Christian.

# 1, A YOUNG MAN CALLED EARLY TO THE WARS

## First Years

Everyone seemed bigger than me. Mother, Father, even my little brother. We had a pet Alsatian called Norris who kept knocking me over, especially when there was mud on the ground. We also had cows and horses which, like the dog, had four legs. I don't believe I saw the top of a horse until my fifth year, they were so huge. I was always worried about keeping out of the way of their feet.

Another little brother. Where did they come from? I worried about being overrun, but at least they were getting smaller. Mother told me I came out of her stomach through a trap door during a snow storm. This seemed incredible even then. One day Norris came limping home, covered with blood and dust. Father said Norris and some other boy dogs had been fighting over a girl dog *in heat*. What was a girl dog? How hot did they get?

I noticed that although I was getting bigger, everyone else was getting bigger, too. For example, the neighbours' boy Petey. Petey would walk over to our house anytime he wanted and punch me out and take my toys. He was unstoppable. I lay awake nights worrying about whether Petey was going to come over the next day and punch me out. Finally I learned to deal with this problem by punching my little brothers and taking their toys. This worked well until Mother caught me. She said I was a bad boy, a trial and a burden, and that she didn't know what had gotten into me. I had to be punished. Father smacked me. It hurt amazingly. Next to horses, Father was the biggest thing in the world.

Chaos. There are boy people *and* girl people! I had to have Mother point out which was which until I got the hang of it myself. Even then, I lay awake nights worrying about making a mistake. And for a long time, I avoided girls because of the heat problem. One day I mentioned this to Father. He laughed and told Mother, and she laughed. Apparently girls were somehow different from dogs in regard to temperature. Relieved of my anxiety on this point, I went over to Petey's place and asked his sister Diane, a girl about my size, to marry me. Diane's mother overheard this unfortunate proposal, called me a fresh little snot and telephoned my parents. I expected a smack when I reached home, but Mother merely took me aside and solemnly told me I was too young to think of marriage. Unaccountably, I felt humiliated by my ignorance on this topic. Who made up the rules?

Petey played with his wee-wee. He told me he had put his hand down Diane's underpants, and she didn't have one. This piece of intelligence filled me with unease. He led me out to the barn and into the calf pen. It was like that, he said, pointing at the hind end of the nearest bawling beast. I wanted to be sick. He took his wee-wee out and started to play with it. I had never seen anything so strange in my whole life. It occurred to me that this was how Diane had lost hers, and I ran home in a panic.

Later I experimented with my brother's to see if the thing was in fact detachable. I was informed on and duly smacked. Mother said I was a monster and nothing but trouble to her. Even at birth, she said, I had tried to come out the wrong way, causing her to be cut open like a bowling bag. I told her I would gladly have gone back if I could, for I had never intended to cause such ruin and shame.

Perhaps, I suggested, I had been born too young and needed a bit more time before breaking into the world. That night I dreamed I was a horse, with Mother and Father and my little brothers running in and out among my hooves like rabbits.

## Kindergarten

I lasted one day only. Had I failed? Later it occurred to me that Mother had withdrawn me from classes for sentimental reasons — she wanted to keep her firstborn by her side an extra year. She wept during the long drive into town. I steeled myself for some dreadful catastrophe. Perhaps they would never let me go home again. She led me down a dark corridor, with doors going off on either side like a hospital, and into a room of strangers. We were both crying by then, and I wouldn't let go of the hem of her skirt. The teacher smiled with a mouth full of teeth, making me wail even louder, for she looked just like the old crone who ate children in my picture book. She pulled my mother and me apart, and sent the light of my life reeling on her way. I expected the chop at any moment and spent the day skulking wherever the other children were thickest, hoping she would take someone else first. And when it was over, I ran screaming from the building in terror to where Mother stood, waiting bravely by the open car door. It took us months to get over the experience.

Meanwhile, she took it upon herself to give me the education I was missing. Numbers. Lord! When I got to fifty, I thought my brains would burst, and yet there didn't seem to be any end to them. I lay awake at night going over them in my head, always worried that the next day I would find out someone had changed the order on me. On the literary side, she taught me phonetics and printing, which

I took to quickly enough, though I pretended to be slow so they would not send me away. School loomed on the horizon like a final separation. What was school? Petey said they gave you the strap at school, which was much worse than a smack. What for? Talking!

## Elementary School

Two-room country schoolhouse. I had my eye out for the strap right away, but on not discovering its location, concluded it was kept in the senior room where the bigger children were no better than wild animals. At recess, I trailed after the student body as it spilled into the yard like a swarm of locusts. Petey raced by shouting, "Don't go near Ted Binker. He stinks." I followed the direction indicated by his pointing finger and spied a lone boy standing in a corner, talking to himself. Out of curiosity, I went over and stood beside him. He did stink. He had wet his pants. I ran after Petey, and someone knocked me down. A little girl in a frilly dress lifted its hem to show me her brown legs and underpants. I went back inside and sat at the wrong desk by mistake. Later I went to the washroom, but couldn't wee-wee because another boy was combing his hair in the mirror. That was my first day.

Miss Barton, my teacher, was young and pretty. I started to play with my wee-wee the way Petey had shown me, imagining that I had accidentally walked in on her in the bathroom. The senior-room teacher was Mr. Kennedy, a giant man with bristly red hair growing out of his ears and nose and on top of his hands. Whenever I saw his hands, I wanted to be sick. Mr. Kennedy gave people the strap. Some of the bigger boys he just walloped with his fist. Once Petey punched Brenda Blandford, and she came to class with thick blood streaming down her chin. Mr. Kennedy picked Petey up and threw him against the art supplies cupboard. Ted Binker wet the floor, but did not get the strap. Petey got the strap twice in one day, once for coming to school with dirty fingernails and once for failing addition. I forgot to do up my pants after going to the bathroom, and Miss Barton asked me if I could feel a draft. I said, no, I felt all right. Then she came over and zipped me up in front of the entire class.

Whaaaa! I failed printing! I connected the letters up the way I had seen Mother do. Mr. Kennedy made me lean against the blackboard on my fingertips for half an hour after school. The next day Mother had a talk with Miss Barton, and they moved me up a grade. In the new grade, everyone was bigger than me. Petey threw my Roy Rogers lunchbox under a truck. Every evening after school, while my brothers played in the yard and Father slept in front of the TV, Mother helped me with my homework. I lay awake nights worrying about failing. I started to pray. I asked God not to let me die while I was asleep and to help me pass addition and bless my dog.

At Christmas, I played Tiny Tim in the school pageant. Father made me a crutch and a leg brace out of tomato soup cans and an old belt. Johnny Malchak carried me on his shoulder, and everyone clapped. Afterwards I tried to wear my leg brace to school so that Mr. Kennedy wouldn't give me the strap. When Mother stopped me wearing the leg brace, I limped.

I noticed that Norris had a shiny wee-wee that came out sometimes. When it did, Mother would hit it with a rolled up newspaper and call Norris a dirty animal. The horse had a giant wee-wee that hung almost to the ground. In my mother's *LIFE MAGAZINE*, I discovered large numbers of photographs of women dressed only in their underwear. I clipped several out with my scissors and showed them to Petey at school. He said that was nothing. In his parents' dresser drawer, he had found the picture of a *nude* woman, only her stomach was covered by a *safe*. I knew that a safe was an iron box where you kept money. I asked Petey why a woman would have a safe on her stomach. Petey said a rubber safe. A rubber safe!

Some nights I didn't sleep at all. There were so many things to worry about. One of the things I worried about was not sleeping. I would get up four or five times to pee, then stand outside my parents' bedroom door until they asked me what was wrong. "I can't sleep," I would say. After I got up to pee and stand outside their door enough times, Mother would come to my room and lie on the bed while I went to sleep. She would be very angry. She said I was neurotic and should see a psychiatrist. She said sometimes she thought there was no hope I would turn out all right. I worried so much about having to see a psychiatrist that I pulled off all my eyelashes. Mother went to see Miss Barton. I expected them to put me back, but Miss Barton gave me a test, and they moved me up another grade. I didn't even know if I passed the test. All the children in the new grade were huge. Petey sat way on the opposite side of the room now. One more grade and I would be in the senior room with Mr. Kennedy.

**Wab-in-hapi**

They sent me to summer camp. Camp Wab-in-hapi. I had to learn new words for everything. The toilet was outside, and it was called the *kaibo*. If you didn't use the right word, they wouldn't let you go. There were eleven other boys in my cabin, none of whom I had ever met before. We all told jokes the first night. A man and a woman are naked together in a bathtub. The man points to the woman's chest and asks, "What are those?" "Mountains," she says. She

points to the hair on his chest and asks, "What's that?"
"Clouds," he says. He points to her stomach and asks,
"What's that?" "My cave," she says. She points to his wee-
wee and asks, "What's that?" "A little man," he says. And
that night the clouds go over the mountains, and the little
man enters the cave. I did not get this joke, but laughed so
that no one would think I was stupid. New words for wee-
wee were *cock, pecker, prick, bone, dink* and *dingus. Fuck* and
*hard-on* I didn't understand, but I found I could get by all
right by laughing whenever anyone used them. I lay awake
most of the first night memorizing words and phrases, so
that the next day I could nonchalantly ask if I might go
take a whiz in the kaibo.

Mornings, at Camp Wab-in-hapi, we lined up for breakfast and sang the camp song. No one told me the words, so
I could only pretend I was singing. I was worried there
might be some rule about not getting to eat if you didn't
sing. Afternoons, the whole camp played War. One side
had to capture the other side's flag. Flags were generally
hidden deep in the woods atop rock outcrops with steep,
dangerous faces. I found the best way to play War was to
hide out somewhere until it was over. The third day somebody hit me over the eye with a rock. I found my cabin
counsellor and told him I was too young for War. That
night the counsellor told my cabin mates I had severe
group adjustment problems. One morning I woke up to
find that the boy in the bunk above had vomited all over
me while I slept. At the end of the week, all the boys in the
camp were ordered to swim naked and wash their wee-wees
with soap. I have never seen so many naked people in my
life.

On Parents' Day, Mother, Father and my brothers visited me. I told them all the jokes I could recall and about
the nice counsellor who wrapped me in his blanket at
campfire and nuzzled my ear. Father said nothing. Mother

said nothing. "In foreign lands," I sang, "the women wear no pants, and the men wear glasses to see their asses." Mother said those were filthy, smutty words. She said I should have my mouth washed out with soap. Father waited till I packed my clothes and we were alone in the car, then he smacked me. "Don't ever let anyone touch you like that again. It's nothing but dirty monkey business."

I told Petey my Wab-in-hapi jokes, and for a while we were friends again. He had taken down Diane's underpants. It was like a pocket, he said. My head whirled. He drew me a diagram which made no sense whatever, though I didn't tell Petey. I memorized the diagram and filed it away with the verbal description *pocket* in that immense portion of my brain set aside for sexual arcana.

At the same time, it occurred to me that many boys of my acquaintance had knowledge far in advance of my own, which they gleaned, more or less scientifically, from their sisters. I began to feel cruelly deprived. I mentioned this casually to Mother, saying how pleasant I imagined it would be when we had a baby girl for me to play with. Mother began to weep. It had been a true wish of her own, she said, to have a daughter, but after my little brothers were born, the doctors had tied her tubes so she would have no more children. The effort of bearing three boys, it seemed, had been highly injurious. I ran out of the house and sat for an hour in the melon patch, till the mosquitoes drove me indoors again. The world was a welter of ignorance, strife and decay.


**Senior Room**


There were nine boys in the senior room, yet because of my size and ineptitude they let Brenda Blandford play third base on the school softball team instead of me. The other boys teased me until I lost my temper and punched Myron Solecki in the nose as hard as I could. This had no effect whatsoever, and I began to stay inside during recess. I played chess with a fat boy named Robert. Anytime during school hours, I could beat Robert handily. But after four o'clock, I would invariably lose. Since then, I have read chess literature extensively without finding a single report of a similar phenomenon. My grades were generally As and Bs, except for Writing, which was always a C. In his written comments, Mr. Kennedy would indicate that I had an attitude problem, which he characterized as, "Daydreams too much. Inattentive. Work sometimes sloppy as a result." I recall that I was beginning to find the presence of girls with breasts disturbing, yet attractive. And I daydreamed constantly about the landing of a vast army of Martian soldiers who recognized me at once as their leader. With my faithful green troops, I conquered the known world and issued undisputed orders such as, "No woman shall wear clothes in the presence of the king."

**High School**

I fainted. That wooden thump during the introduction of the new teachers was my head hitting the gym floor. Only six hundred and eighty-two strangers noticed. I was carried to the principal's office, where the school secretary put wet paper towels on the back of my neck while I sat with my head between my knees. Life was over. At twelve, I had nothing to look forward to but the grave.

There were several large-breasted girls in my new class, but none of them seemed interested in me because of my size and youth. I tried out for the football team my second week. Someone hit me in the stomach with a ball, knocking the wind out of me. Huge boys, as big as horses, ran over my body as I lay gasping in the dirt. Petey said I was lucky to be in high school. He said some of the girls in my class went *all the way*. One I liked especially, because she seemed so quiet and sweet, Petey had seen in a parked car with a boy from the football team. The boy had had his hand inside her blouse. Hearing this, I felt betrayed.

I played with my wee-wee so much I gave myself a blister. I thought it was finally going to drop off. Mother came to my room and asked me if I were unhappy. I said no, but she seemed suddenly thoughtful. I screamed, "Don't let them put me ahead another grade!" Instead, she took me to see a psychiatrist. The whole day I took tests. I had to answer questions like "What are your spare-time activities?" and "If Bill is Bob's brother and Jean is Bob's mother and Emily is Bill's aunt and Jean and Emily are not sisters, how is Bill related to Jean?" I sweated pools worrying over what they would do if I failed. When it was all over, the psychiatrist told Mother I had a "near genius" I.Q. His preference survey showed that I would make an excellent "concert penis." I was mortified hearing that word spoken in front of my mother and tried desperately to make her hurry away. Unaccountably, the news seemed to cheer her up. She bought me a milkshake on the way home and said I was a good little boy who would make her proud. I began to take piano lessons after school, though it was obvious from the start I had no talent.

Winter came and I asked the sweet, quiet girl to go to the Christmas dance with me. To be on the safe side, in case of cancellations, I asked a half-dozen other girls as well. Apparently this was a *faux pas*. My mother finally arranged a date for me with a little girl named Wanda Welbourne who was still in elementary school but only a year older than me. It wasn't until Father had picked her up and driven us to the high school that I realized Mother had made a terrible mistake. Wanda refused to dance with me, not because she was shy, but on religious grounds. Her minister, she said, believed that God kept a watchful eye on high school dance floors. We sat in the bleachers the whole evening drinking Cokes. Every twenty minutes or so, Wanda would go to the bathroom with a group of other girls. They all wore crinolines that snapped as they walked, and the smell of their perfume made me dizzy. Later, when I walked Wanda to her door, I tried to kiss her cheek. Suddenly, she grabbed me. He mouth opened like a great hole, and she stuck out her stomach so that I nearly lost my balance. I put my hand on her breast. "No, no!" she said, wrenching herself away and shutting the door between us. I reeled down the walk to my father's car, sure that he had seen everything.

**Piano Lessons**

The next year I was an inch taller and tried to impress people by giving myself the nickname "Moose" which did not catch on. Wanda Welbourne told everyone I was her boyfriend, although I had not seen her since Christmas. Petey had somehow made it to high school. He told me he'd heard Wanda had legs like peanut butter. "What do you mean?" I asked. "They spread easy." I still did not understand jokes. I made the football team because, as it happened, Wanda's father was the assistant coach. I was knocked out the first week. The second week I fainted when someone stepped on my hand with his cleated boots.

Fridays, after school, I walked across town to take my piano lesson. My teacher was Mrs. Crotty. She kept a photograph of her dead husband on top of the piano next to the sheet music and made me play with oranges balanced on top of my hands. (If you try this, you will see that it is impossible.) The best thing about piano lessons was Sylvia

Tandino who lived in house at the end of Mrs. Crotty's street. Every Friday, Sylvia and I would spend the one-hour interval between school and my piano lesson upstairs in her bedroom studying, with a complete set of the *Encyclopedia Britannica* propped against the door. Sylvia's mother, a young Italian widow who worked afternoons at the pickle factory, never bothered us. We would lie on the bed, wrapped in each other's arms, while Sylvia taught me to French kiss. It was Sylvia who said, "When I was a little girl, I thought babies come out where you shit. Imagine that!" Thus putting paid to another misconception I had entertained following Petey's barnyard demonstrations.

One Friday, Wanda Welbourne invited me to her house to play Monopoly prior to my piano lesson. We had Cokes and iced cupcakes in the Welbournes' rec room. Wanda pulled me down on top of her on the fire resistant carpet, nearly crushing me with her arms. When she kissed me, our teeth knocked together so hard I was afraid we had chipped them. She rubbed her stomach against me until I was quite delirious and pushed my hand up under her skirt from behind. "I love this," she whispered, adding after a moment, "I mean, I love you." I was trying to slip my fingers inside the band of her underpants, when she suddenly threw me off, twisting my arm and impaling my back on a Monopoly piece.

**Adultery**

There was nothing left but work and study! Sylvia and Wanda had a fight over me in the girls' change room during PT. Wanda won. I was her boyfriend again. But she wouldn't have anything to do with me, claiming that I had committed adultery. Adultery! Sylvia cried when she returned my Dylan albums. I felt guilt twist in my stomach

when I saw her tears. At the same time, I couldn't help but
be amazed at Wanda's perfidiousness. The woman would
stop at nothing to get what she wanted. She had turned everyone against me — only Petey continued to be my friend.

For several weeks I swore off girls and devoted myself to
physical culture, doing sit-ups and push-ups every night
before going to bed. I vowed to stop playing with my wee-
wee. Petey discovered a stack of black and white photos of
naked people in his parents' dresser drawer. One showed a
pretty woman with a man's wee-wee in her mouth. Another
showed the same woman with her legs stretched apart, her
crotch hidden in a thatch of tightly coiled hair. Petey read
me passages from a book called *Peyton Place.* I was shocked
to find it had been written by a woman named Grace. The
pictures and words confused me so much that I broke my
vow. All I could think about was the woman in the photograph. In desperation, I asked Wanda to the Christmas
dance, our second date. She said no, that we must go sepa-
rately as part of my punishment, but that we might sit
together on the bleachers and talk.

I sat on the bleachers for two hours, sipping Coke.
Wanda arrived with her older brother and his girlfriend
and immediately disappeared into the bathroom. Later I
saw her kissing someone under the mistletoe. Petey had
come to the dance alone with a branch of mistletoe and
was wandering around bothering girls. He even tried to
kiss Miss Demian, the algebra teacher. Wanda walked in
front of the bleachers with three other girls, laughing. I
heard her whisper the word "bigamist" as they passed.
Petey chased Wanda and her friends shrieking into the
bathroom, then came and offered me a drink of his Coke.
When I shook my head, he said, "This isn't Coke, you
dummy. This is a mickey. I got a whole six-pack outside,
too." I took a sip and coughed until I thought my throat
was bleeding. Petey followed Miss Demian without her no-

ticing, holding his hands up under her bottom, pretending to catch her turds. He caught Wanda under the mistletoe and kissed her for ten minutes or so. I drank the rest of his Coke and went outside to be sick, having experienced the true emptiness and solitude of the life of passion. I decided that I was probably turning into an alcoholic.

**Love**

Sylvia let me touch her breasts. This after prolonged negotiation, some of which we conducted over the telephone. My mother must have overheard, for under my pillow one night, I discovered a paperback volume entitled *Family Life for Teens*. *Family Life* came replete with tasteful photographs and line diagrams accompanied by inane captions like "Puppy Love" (the picture of a boy and girl squeezed together on a playground swing) and "Female Reproductive Organs" (a vague sketch that reminded me of two garden beans sprouting side by side in a glass of water). From *Family Life*, I learned that Sylvia and I were engaged in petting, which until then was something I thought you did to a dog. After petting came heavy petting, which apparently was dangerous as it could lead to the girl having a baby. How this happened I could not quite make out from the text and diagrams. Now, when my father drove me into town for a school dance or a party, he would look at me sternly before I got out of the car and say, "I hope you won't do anything that will make us ashamed of you." At such times, I felt under tremendous pressure as I did not know what he meant, though I hoped I would measure up.

Sylvia and I began to flaunt our sexuality. In class we would scribble passionate love notes punctuated with jealous directives against so much as looking at members of the opposite sex. We would exchange adoring glances, sometimes sticking out the tips of our tongues to indicate that we wanted to French kiss. Miss Demian caught us one day. When the period was over, she took me aside and advised me in the sternest terms that seeing too much of one person could lead to trouble. What sort of trouble? Mrs. Crotty began to remark on my late arrivals, my often sweaty state when I did arrive after running all the way from Sylvia's house, and my complete inattention. She had given up on the oranges and pressed me through the first three Conservatory grades without allowing me to endure the inevitable disillusionment of examination. My mother began to be cross with me for not practising and threatened to stop paying for my lessons. Music had turned out to be a grave disappointment to her. It was also mentioned that my psychiatric assessment had cost Father $150 — "all for nothing."

When I played with my wee-wee, I thought about every woman I knew, even Mrs. Crotty and Miss Demian. *Family Life* said that playing with my wee-wee (penis) was called masturbation, that many boys did it (had my mother read this?) and that it would stop after marriage. There were several popular misconceptions regarding masturbation: for example, it could make you go mad or blind or grow hair on the palms of your hands. I had not heard this before and wondered if it might be true. There *was* hair growing on the *backs* of my hands! I proposed to Sylvia that we have intercourse to prevent me from going bonkers before I got out of Grade 10. She declined, but continued to allow me to touch her breasts. I attempted forays toward what *Peyton Place* called "the vee of her crotch." We made so much noise that Mrs. Tandino's new boyfriend, Ray, came upstairs one afternoon and tried to push the bedroom door open against the stack of encyclopedias.

All this persecution served only to make our love grow

stronger. We read *Romeo and Juliet* in English that year. I saw the movie — the bedroom scene made me light-headed, though I noted that Sylvia's breasts were not as large as Juliet's. I discovered that Sylvia often wore a combination girdle and garter belt. She let me touch between her legs as long as I kept my hands outside the girdle. We went to see a movie together, and she masturbated me through my pants in the back row. As far as I can tell, no one has ever written about the problem of wet pants in young love. Yet, along with the pleasure, I began to feel a nagging guilt for the secret life we were leading. I was turning into a split personality like Jekyll and Hyde.

## Fatherhood

I suffered a nervous breakdown! All I could do was lie in bed and sleep. My mother said I had been doing too much, what with football, drama club, choir, United Nations club, math club, piano and ballroom dancing lessons — all of which she'd forced me to endure (except for the football). But that wasn't the real reason. I was a father! At least Sylvia said I was. She wasn't sure. This announcement came the afternoon Coach Welbourne let me run a play when both our first and second string quarterbacks were injured. I fumbled and then recovered for no yards, but at least I had been on the field. Between the game and my drama club rehearsal, Sylvia said her period was late. How late? A day. A day! I saw my career as a professional ballplayer vanish like a mirage. Suddenly, I had to make plans and be responsible. We would live with my parents until I was sixteen, then move away someplace where I could get a job as a checkout boy or a truck driver (if my father would teach me to drive).

Everything seemed shrouded in a dead, gray cloud — I

knew how much my parents would be disappointed. Mother was already disturbed because I had abandoned Wanda for Sylvia Tandino. She told me I was becoming common. Though we might have crushes on a variety of people as we grew up, she said, it was better to marry a person from the same background. Sylvia was a nice girl, but she had never enjoyed the advantages I had. Also she was Catholic and we were Anglican. I said Sylvia made me happy. Mother said one had to be awfully careful to ensure long-term happiness. Her arguments seemed well-meant and kindly, but they made me feel uncomfortable.

Sylvia went to a doctor for tests. For the week we had to wait for the results, I remained in bed. Mother said I had a work-avoidance neurosis. Father said I was lazy. I could not face the world. My future hung in the balance. I was only a child myself. How could a child have a child? This was God's punishment for playing with my penis and not listening to my parents. The night before the test results were due, I confessed everything. I knew by then there was no hope for one so mired in sin as I was. Besides, my parents would need to make arrangements for Sylvia to move in. Probably my brothers would have to double up so she could have one of their rooms.


**Afterward**


I am fifteen now. Old. In a year, I will be able to get my driver's licence. Sylvia was not pregnant. But she had to tell the doctor who she had had intercourse with. The doctor said, "He's so young. I didn't think he was man enough." I chose to regard this as a compliment. Sylvia and I have agreed to have a chaste relationship from now on and begin to see other people. I feel the adult world closing in

— those brief hours of freedom before Mrs. Crotty's lesson are no more. My musical career also has ended. Many things have changed. Petey's sister Diane got pregnant in Grade 9. Petey took it hard and now is in reform school for arson. Sylvia has found part-time work as an office assistant for the doctor who gave her the pregnancy test. The doctor has taken down his pants in front of her and invited her to go to Acapulco with him (he was only married a year ago!) during the Christmas holidays. Wanda has become a lesbian and cut her hair short. So far I don't think she has found any other lesbians in our school — perhaps she is only doing this to draw attention to herself.

The other day Mother and Father had a fight. Mother confided to me that Father had ruined the whole birth experience for her by saying he would be embarrassed if she screamed. Apparently, Mother had been looking forward to screaming. One begins (I am beginning) to realize how wounded everyone is, how many wounds there are. In my dreams, the future bears down upon me like a runaway horse.

# THE TRAVESTY OF SLEEP

Far into the travesty of sleep we are making tracks
for higher ground.
> — T.C. Cannon, Caddo Indian artist
> killed in a car accident in the plaza
> at Santa Fe, 1979.

## The Worm

I was in Santa Fe the spring the prisoners rioted.

That was a terrible situation as you may recall. Prisoners broke into the pharmacy and took all the drugs, then tortured snitches and queers to death and burned buildings down around their ears. The State of New Mexico called in the National Guard. I remember uniformed soldiers racing through the streets to muster-points, olive-green Medivac helicopters ferrying the dead and injured to the hospital on St. Michael's Drive, smoke rising from the mesa below the city and TV reporters wading through the ruined cell blocks in rubber boots, speaking smugly of horrible things.

One incident the TV reporters liked especially to tell about was the discovery of a man who had been burned to death with acetylene torches, then had his head chopped off and stuck between his legs.

For days there were rumours that prisoners remained unaccounted for, that they were either ashes under the collapsed gymnasium roof or had somehow escaped into the

Sangre de Cristo Mountains where they lived in caves long since abandoned by the Indians.

On Good Friday, I drove to Chimayo with a friend. We entered the Sanctuario to dig a handful of holy mud from the mysterious hole in the sacristy and saw the glass-encased statues of the Infant Jesus and the Virgin of Prague, the primitive religious paintings hanging along the walls, and all the prayerful, hand-written messages left there by simple folk.

> Dear Baby Jesus, Take care of my brother Ramon who is in the prison and we have not heard from him.

Outside the church, I threw my holy mud (now dried to sand) away, though some continued to cling to the lines in my palm and beneath my fingernails.

I wondered about Ramon, where he was and what terrible crime he had committed, or not committed. I wondered if Ramon were the man with his head off and his own cock in his mouth, like the snake biting its tail or like the Worm of Ouroboros, the worm of the world.

Or if he had become ashes on the wind.

Somehow I did not see him as one of those who managed to survive by staying out in the prison yard, under the search lights night after night, while the buildings rang with shrieks and moans and cries of ecstasy.

Or, I asked myself, had he climbed through a gap in the wire fence, hidden from the search lights by night and the billowing smoke which ascended from the pyres of bodies and mattresses?

In the sunlight at Chimayo, with the passionate worshippers gathering to celebrate the death and resurrection of Jesus (a man about my age who died in Palestine two thousand years ago; also, I conjecture, about Ramon's age;

also a prisoner — we must all seek release in our own way, or we must all seek transformation, that is what I say, we must transform ourselves whatever the cost), with the lines of passionate pilgrims hiking up the roads to Chimayo bearing their palms and crosses, passing the little white crosses and bundles of plastic flowers (shrines to motor vehicle accidents), with all this, shall we say, excessive religiosity going on around me and my companion, the Angel of Death (Doña Sebastiana, she of the death cart, with bow and arrow, in the museum at Taos — I will explain this later), frowning at me for throwing the mud away, as if my lack of faith somehow cast doubt on her own belief (we must all be pilgrims together say the sheep and the shepherds), with all this going on, I am thinking quite passionately myself about Ramon slipping like a wraith along the mesa, hiding beneath pinyon trees as the sun comes up, drinking his own urine in the heat, searching for a cave to lie up in, perhaps with a lion or a rattlesnake.

Brother of the rattlesnake.

I imagine — this is what I would have done, and have I not made it clear already that I see Ramon, no doubt a petty drug dealer awaiting trial, as a doppelganger, my other (better) self, the one who manages to break out, to evade, escape, translate? — I imagine that he has taken care to throw his captors off his trail.

Perhaps he found a body (I am nearly positive it was Ramon who arranged the man-biting-his-own-penis image; he is that sort, a desperate rogue with a biting sense of humour), somewhat the analogue of his own (we cannot escape, or make art, without this curious doubling), and used the acetylene torch to destroy its facial features and fingerpads. (This is gruesome, some of the worst killers in that prison are momentarily sobered and frightened by Ramon's single-minded indifference; they back away in awe, then splash giggling down the corridors.)

The teeth he smashed out with a ballpeen hammer, then ground into a fine dust and scattered over the sewage water running at his feet. (Once you decide to escape, to change yourself, you must be ruthless, you cannot be afraid — and besides, the man was dead, or at least unconscious, before Ramon began.)

I don't blame him at all. Circumstances had driven him mad, the prison, the hideous tribal retaliations, the images of torture and the walls that kept him in there, and the thought of his sister weeping, wringing her handkerchief in the kitchen beneath a picture of the Sacred Heart. (The note's hand had been female, a pious young woman's writing — already I am a little in love with her and plan, as Ramon and I flee together over the Blood of Christ Mountains, disguised, yes, as priests, to become better acquainted when we meet her to exchange news and acquire money and food.)

The woman I am with disapproves of my lack of faith and my sexual preference (like Ramon, I am a homosexual, one of those in the prison they like to rape with their fists, then kill). She thinks she can save me, would like to get me into bed.

She thinks I am the kind of man she could settle with for a while — this, I hasten to add, is an impression resulting from the fact that I listen to her uncritically, which is something many women miss in a man. And I like her, find her interesting. This is terribly flattering (considering the life she's led) and it's almost enough to make her fall in love with me. So, when I throw away the holy mud, it is as if I am throwing away her (mud) heart.

Everything is symbolic, you see. And I signify my petty rebellion by reversal, loving the mirror's reflection, not the other.

It was her idea to come to Chimayo — and, believe me, I am grateful. This Ramon connection is more than I could have hoped for.

Absently I scan the nearby mountains, imagining that I might spy him there, a naked man (he had to get rid of the prison clothes first thing; the prime rule of transformation is you must go naked, you must leave everything behind).

Without his clothes and with his identity left behind with that poor, mutilated corpse (after everything, he consigned it to the pyre), he is a new man up there on the mountainside.

He looked down at us with an other-worldly curiosity. Who are these strange creatures, these boxes that move and don't, their antennae waving in the sunsets?

It is my theory that the prison is the representative image of the modern world. You'll recall that Shakespeare let his characters strut their moment upon the stage. But nowadays we are inside a prison, the walls of a labyrinth, and there is no outside, or outside is madness and Ramon. I exult and wave to the hills. I lift up mine eyes unto the hills.

But the hills don't answer.


**New Life Forms**

My friend's name is Esmé Altschuler. I call her the Angel of Death because that is the work she does. She hires herself out to sit with the dying. When they see my friend coming through the door, these people know it is the end. Some welcome it. She will call me during her lunch break. In the background, sometimes drowning out her words, I will hear the moans and grunts of the dying. What's that? I ask, trembling. That's just Bruce, she says, and goes on telling me the gossip.

Bruce is a retired movie executive dying of prostate cancer.

Esmé's calling me from the deathbed; Bruce hears everything she says.

Esmé's from Chicago. Her first lover was a boy named Leopoldo, the son of an Argentinian diplomat. They made love in the ruins of a condemned tenement, in the dust and broken bricks. Her father was an alcoholic, and she recalls the day he left for good, when she was eight and had just climbed to the crotch of an oak tree in their yard. She watched her father walk out to his car with a suitcase in each hand.

Esmé married a man who does biological research, inventing new life forms. I met him once, in a bar called Richard's Horseman's Haven out by the race track, where we had a long, drunken conversation about the possibility of some of these life forms escaping. He said it was entirely probable that some had already done so. Generally, they would be too weak to survive in the real world, he said. They could not sustain themselves against everyday diseases or the attacks of higher animals or heat or cold.

Esmé and the biologist came west to New Mexico together and then divorced.

She married a Vietnam veteran and joined the Divine Light Mission. They lived in an A-frame near Taos. Twice they gave away everything they owned on the whim of their guru. After the second time, Esmé drifted south to Santa Fe, looking for another kind of light.

She studies at the Santa Fe School of Natural Medicine, things like massage technique and herbal remedies. She lives with two other students in a bungalow in the Spanish barrio behind the deaf school. She smells of saffron. Hanging over the shower curtain rod in their bathroom are the rubber tubes and bladders of three enema kits.

The Angel of Death.

Esmé and her friends eat peyote and take turns lying naked in the bathtub.

They give themselves enemas and see gods.

She wants to sleep with me.

I smell saffron and hear Bruce's grunts (his screams inhabit my dreams).

I think of the image of Doña Sebastiana, mounted on a cart, a bow and arrow in her hands, in the Taos Museum and the strange, wooden Cristo behind the reredos in the church at Las Trampas, the Cristo with His ribs carved outside His chest, that look of mortified agony on His face, His body riding upon the nails.

## Spanish Boys

When we drive down from Chimayo, it is night. East of the road, the Sangre de Cristos are tumescent and silver, sharp against the clear, moonlit sky. Westward, clouds creep over the Jemez and lightning bolts shatter against the slopes like glass rods.

I think of my friend Larry, a stained-glass artist from San Francisco. Larry can't find work in Santa Fe except as a labourer. He spends his days scraping bark from redwood logs to make the natural-looking beams contractors use in the modern adobe subdivisions out on the mesa.

Nights Larry wears black velvet gloves to hide his hands.

Nights he and I go to La Fonda to listen to a Panamanian salsa band and dance with the Spanish stenographers. (Two of the musicians are ex-priests and gay — they tell of a huge monastery in the mountains where bent priests from all over the country go to be purified or hidden; the drunk priests, mad priests, promiscuous, gay and pederastic priests, the sinful men of God — I don't know if this is true.)

From time to time Larry disappears, and I know he is downstairs in the basement men's room, having sex in the cubicles.

When I go down there to pee, there is always a Spanish boy at the next urinal asking me for taxi fare home, or a man sitting in a cubicle with his trousers down and the door open.

These Spanish boys have a difficult time. They are expected to be macho womanizers and, at home, in the towns and villages around Santa Fe, they act the role. But nights they sneak into the city for sex with white men, to bars like the Senate, the Gold Bar or La Fonda (La Fonda is the safest because a lot of women go there).

Outside, other Spanish boys in low-riding cars squeal their tires and toss beer bottles at the queers in the streets.

The boys are quick, passionate lovers; the sense of sin, of being lost to the world, of going down into the depths, of giving up, is a kind of transformation for them.

Spanish boys know something about miracles and evil.


**Brothers of Light**

This is in Santa Fe, New Mexico, as I have said.

Forty miles away at Los Alamos, men like Esmé's husband, with degrees from Harvard and M.I.T., are building bombs and fusion reactors and components for machines that will travel in outer space. At a museum there, they have exact replicas of Fat Man and Little Boy, the bombs dropped on Hiroshima and Nagasaki. The tour guides at the museum are wives of research physicists — even the wives have Ph.D.s.

Once in a Los Alamos bar, I met a retired army sergeant who had witnessed thirty-three atomic bomb tests, crouching as close as a mile from Ground Zero. (Note the numerological correspondence — Jesus was thirty-three when he died; it is Easter; I am thirty-three.) His greatest regret was missing the first detonation at Trinity in White Sands because of the flu.

Dotting the mesa roundabout are the ruins of ancient Indian villages called pueblos. Sometimes, at places like Puye and Tsankawi, you stand atop the cliffs amid the ruins like a man on the prow of a ship, surveying the vast pinyon country where these people once grew their crops of maize and beans.

Contemporary pueblos have Catholic churches and little adobe-walled cemeteries crowded with white wooden crosses. But the Indians (they survive by adopting the disguise of the other) also preserve the kivas of their own religion. As the calendar rolls around, they hold their seasonal rites and dances: the corn dance, the cloud dance, the buffalo dance.

I have seen these — at San Ildefonso, Tesuque, Santo Domingo — it is like seeing the cave paintings at Lascaux, it is like seeing the animal masters calling their prey.

They dream of the day when the buffalo will return.

In the mountains between Santa Fe and Taos, I have driven through picturesque run-down Spanish villages with names like Cordova, Truchas, Ojo Sarcas, Chamisal and Las Trampas. Each village has a morada, an unprepossessing chapel (adobe, with no windows, strangely prison-like) where Los Hermanos Penitentes, Los Hermanos de Luz, the Brothers of Light, hold their cruel medieval rites, whipping one another (at Easter especially), and at night marching through the streets carrying wooden crosses.

In days gone by, it is said, they would crucify a man, taking him down from the cross before he died, in commemoration of the passion of Christ.

A human Cristo, image of Christ.

I am fascinated by these believers. I think particularly of the men chosen to act the part of Jesus, the ones who are crucified.

Once Larry (an indefatigable and promiscuous lover) met a Spanish boy who invited him to a Penitente Easter service. He sat with his friend, amid the congregation, listening to the strange hymns and litany, the eerie pitero pipes. In the next room, hidden from the worshippers, the brothers were whipping themselves with yucca cactus spines. Larry could hear the sound of the whips falling. At the instant of tenieblas, when the candles were snuffed and a shout rose and the sound of whirling bull-roarers (metracas) filled the air, Larry observed an old woman fall to the floor in a fit or a swoon.

The rest of the congregation ignored her. Larry had no idea what he should do. For all he knew, she could have been choking to death or having a heart attack. He knelt and felt her pulse, then grasping her wrists, dragged her into the darkness outside and gave her the kiss of life. Just as shouting and roaring subsided and the brothers relit the candles inside the morada, the woman began to spit up and moan.

Faces (chalky white, he says, with eyes like coal or chips of obsidian) appeared in the doorway. "A devil!" they shouted. "A devil!" Larry's friend tried to lead him away by the hand, but he stood there a moment, confused and unnerved, while Los Hermanos railed at him, shoving him with their fists and whip handles. When they began to collect stones to throw, Larry fled, racing through the streets after his lover, with shouts of "Devil! Devil!" following him and stones clattering on the pavement.

Larry says Los Hermanos thought she was dead. They thought only the devil or some powerful sorcerer could bring that woman back to life.

I think of Larry bringing the dead woman to life and being stoned for making miracles and the man who becomes Christ on the cross. I think of Ramon in the hills fleeing his walled Jerusalem. I think of the Indians dressed in animal skins and the transformations of the atom. (Hiking in the Bandelier Forest, Esmé and I picked up shards of pottery a thousand years old and, at the same moment, heard muffled explosions from nearby canyon test sites.)

I think of Ramon, who is me, stumbling into a Penitente village, finding himself petted, healed and fed. Perhaps they bring a young, beautiful girl for him to lie with. Then in the night, the Brothers come for him with their nails. The man who has escaped the hell of the prison (Jerusalem) finds himself spread out upon the boards. Screaming, he feels the spikes spread the bones of his hands, the flesh tear. He did not kill the man, he shouts. He is innocent.

The Brothers shake their heads sagely; their expressions are passionate and beatific. They pound the nails and whip themselves in a frenzy. The bull-roarers whirl. The yucca thorns dig into Ramon's scalp and forehead.

Screaming, he goes out of himself. His soul goes up to the stars.

His atoms recombine in new ways.

Huge amounts of energy are released.

A mushroom cloud rises above the spot (Trinity).

Hymns rise to the heavens.

The world is transformed.

It becomes worse.

Somewhere his sister wakes from a cruel sleep, feeling the wounds in her hands and feet and side. She wakes screaming. She prays to the Baby Jesus. She thinks a miracle has occurred.

## Carreta del Muerto

I sleep with Esmé, the Angel of You Know What.

It's not so bad.

Perhaps the holy mud from the Sanctuario has worked its rude magic. I remember a verse from a Penitente hymn.

> Esta vida es un ungano,
> Y nos tiene con desvelo,
> Y los eres invertidos
> Para sustentar el duelo.

In bed we talk about the impossibility of freedom in the industrial age. I hazard the opinion that my sexual ambiguity, my love for Larry, my moods, caprices, depressions, neuroses and suicidal tendencies are signs of moral worth in an age ruled by technocracy.

The bed smells of saffron, death and vaginal secretions. The sheets rustle as we move. In the bathroom, I smell the stale rubberiness of enema bags.

Esmé (a.k.a. Death, Doña Sebastiana, Hecate, the Virgin Mary, Clytemnestra, Cassandra, Jocasta, Isis, the Wicked Witch of the West and my mother) crouches above me in a kind of triumph, touching herself with fingers she moistens on her tongue. I close my eyes and let my hands explore the alien contours of her breasts, the corrugations of her rib cage, the mysterious angles of her belly. I touch the hand touching herself, wondering where her mind is (her eyes are closed), what her pleasure is like.

I think all love is this solitary riding, and we never touch each other.

I think (of course) of Ramon's sister, with her black velvet gloves, the stigmata and her starved, waxen body (I conjure her from old lovers and books), a hot ventricle for the reception of my (arrow) cock. She is so thin; she is all eyes and hands and feet. Her turgid nipples, black like eyes in the moonlight, scrape against my chest and draw blood. Her body smells of rubber. (The invisible woman is the real woman.)

The death cart in the museum at Taos is a low wooden wagon with solid wheels like the old ox-carts. Doña Sebastiana is a small, rubbery figure, clothed in a black dress, with staring, coal-black eyes and a chalky face. In her hands, she holds a drawn bow and arrow. It is said that sometimes, as the cart is dragged through the streets, the jostling of the wooden wheels causes the bow to release; the arrow flies and whoever it touches dies.

Concealed about the cart under Death's skirts and petticoats are other primitive instruments of execution — an ax-head, a stone hammer, a heavy rock.

Sometimes Death's eyes are covered to symbolize her blind uncertainty.

When the Indians dance, they wear skunk-fur anklets to ward off evil spirits. Everywhere their feet touch the ground, it is sacred soil.

Los Hermanos de Luz have their Campo Santo.

The physicists of Los Alamos are said to sublimate their fears in wife-swapping orgies and sado-masochistic sex games. All this comes out whenever there is a divorce; Los Alamos divorces are notorious in Santa Fe legal circles. No one wants to settle out of court. Spouses can't wait to get on the witness stand and divulge their dirty secrets.

The physicists at Los Alamos are trying to transmute elements; they are trying to build engines that make their own fuel; they are trying to travel in time and render themselves immortal.

Like them, I do not know where I am safe.

All this is alien to Ramon who has escaped, fled, translated himself out of culture, who has died (albeit symbolically). It is night (the night of our visit to Chimayo, an indeterminate number of nights after his disappearance from the prison) and he has acquired an immateriality which renders him invisible.

Nights, his sister waits anxiously for a call, her car loaded with food, medicine, money and our monkish disguises. Just as now, during the Feast of Easter, wives and lovers pack their cars with food and warm clothing and drive along the highways to succour the pilgrims marching toward Chimayo with their Cristos, Madonnas and Santos.

This immateriality has its own terror; Ramon travels barefoot in the mountain snows with his hair perpetually on end. He has left the hell of his prison, which at least possessed a certain interior logic, for a hell of the spirit, the shocking emptiness of his freedom. He craves food, love, sex, wine, pain, birth and death. He feels a crushing nostalgia for the certainty of desire and walls. But that's all gone now. He lives on pinyon nuts left by the squirrels or maize cobs abandoned in ancient pueblo warehouses. He tries to kill a coyote, but the animal twists its back like a trout and disappears through his fingers.

To survive, in order not to succumb to the elements, he needs a new vocabulary.

Esmé comes with a sigh. She crosses her hands over her belly and rocks with pleasure.

Her preoccupation with death repels and fascinates me. I do not know if what I feel for her is love (I am certain with Larry, for example) or if I am merely attracted by her oddity, her history. Doña Sebastiana.

I put my hand down there and smell my fingers. Everything smells of old, rotten rubber. I lock myself in the bathroom, rip the shower curtain from its rod, upset the medicine shelf into the sink and tie an enema tube around my neck so that the bladder flops against my chest. I smash the mirror with a jar of Noxema. Esmé weeps in the hallway. I take a shard of glass and examine myself in its incomplete and inaccurate reflection.

My feet are bleeding.

I realize that I am prey to dualisms, diagrams and allegories which are only masks for the truth, that my truth is nothing but an obsessive topological assault upon reality.

My feet are bleeding.

This is what I think: failure reveals intention. Certain questions cannot be asked, let alone answered. We kill what we love, we love what we cannot have, we destroy ourselves pursuing illusions we cannot live without.

**Jornada del Muerto**

I am feeling a little on edge.

I have used a shard of mirror glass to slit a hole in the shower curtain, which, draped over my shoulders, forms a kind of poncho, ideal in case of rain. I wear the enema bag like a neck-tie. The other two enema bags I have fastened around my ankles where they drag as I walk.

My bandaged feet no longer fit properly inside my shoes. It is difficult (a combination of sore feet and tangled enema bags) for me operate the pedals of Esmé's car. There are shooting pains in my palms. I can't get the image of the dead man with his head between his legs out of my mind. He is like some mythic constellation placed in the heavens as my guide.

Certain things begin to make sense to me — for example, Edwin Hubble's discovery in 1929 that the galaxies are moving away from each other and the abrupt extinctions at the end of the Triassic period.

I drive to Larry's place, having some trouble with the manual stick-shift which turns out to be automatic.

Ramon has been here before me.

The window next to the corner fireplace in Larry's room has been smashed inward. Shards of glass, smashed pottery bowls, Larry's sketches of Mimbres pot designs and broken kachina dolls litter the floor. Rocks the size of grapefruit are everywhere. I think of the word *erratics,* which geologists use to refer to stones bulldozed and left in odd places by glaciers. Larry is naked on the bed, his body a pattern of blackened welts, bruises and lesions, his eyes open and his jaw slack. Cold air blows in through the window. The air smells like stale rubber. Larry's arms are stretched out at his sides, one foot covers the other, one knee is slightly flexed. His anorexic torso seems carved from wax. His gray rib bones look as though they have worn right through his skin.

I am relieved to see no signs of stigmata.

Snow blows through the open window. My shower curtain poncho is no protection against the cold. My feet leave marks on the floor. The enema bag anklets drag behind me, defining the zone of safety.

> A! que penosa jornada,
> Que camino tan atros!
> Me voy para la otra vida
> Lo determina mi Dios.

Nothing surprises me.

Only the week before, worshippers at the little church in Mora claimed to see Jesus' face outlined in the adobe plaster of the nave wall.

I have heard tales of a renegade Charismatic priest who

travels through the remote Spanish villages healing the sick with his hot hands.

I can think of only one possible ethical rule: live with the maximum intensity.

On a mountainside not far off, Ramon lifts his head and howls. He is a soul in torment. His pace quickens as he rushes toward the place of assignation. He has (of course) lost all sense of direction. His bare feet go slap-slap along ancient Indian trails worn deep into the soft tuff-rock, leaving little bloody toe prints.

I pick up a crumpled piece of paper from the floor. It's a mailer from a gay group Larry belongs to. The publishers profess to have started a homosexual religion. The paper is printed with a depiction of their man-god: a bearded male, seated in the lotus position, with a huge, erect phallus rising from his lap. His palms are pressed together as if in prayer. He has antlers growing out of his temples. I recognize in the man's face the lineaments of my own.

I touch Larry's cold toes. Once he brought an old woman back to life with a kiss and was mistaken for the devil. He moans a little and makes a smacking sound with his lips. He looks just like me. With the moustaches, we could pass for brothers. I find the black gloves with his glasses on the bedside table.

Slowly, piece by piece, I am taking on the guise of another.

There is something dreadful in all this. I have a deep yearning to get back to solid ground instead of sinking every step, as it were, into the quicksand of semiotic equivalencies.

I think of Ramon and what has happened to Larry.

Everything that is of the Absolute is evil.

The rocks in Larry's room have a strangely metallic quality which I associate with meteorites. I think of the

danger of meteorite showers (common events at high alti-
tude), thankful that I am wearing a shower curtain.

The phrase *assaulted by words* comes to mind.

I notice that each of the rocks has a word chiselled into
its surface. Turning over the nearest ones with my feet, I
read the words, "Turning over the nearest ones with my
feet, I read the words, 'Turning over the nearest ones with
my feet, I read the words . . .

## Black Mesa, or the Future

I notice that the back seat of Esmé's car has been packed as
if for a long journey: sleeping bags, backpacks, freeze-dried
food, a short-wave radio, canteens, a bottle of whisky, a
Bible with several passages marked and the monk's habit
disguises.

With a clarity that is like the heat flash of an atomic
bomb, I recall the initial message, the sister's prayer.

> Dear Baby Jesus, Take care of my brother
> Ramon who is in the prison and we have not
> heard from him.

Esmé greets me at her door with a sour look and then
begins to weep.

Standing in her living room, with the Chimayo blankets
hanging from the walls and the smell of saffron everywhere, I begin to predict the future.

Esmé will marry a man named Volk who already has a
child by another marriage. They will move to Spearfish,
S.D., where she will be no happier than she has a right to
be.

Larry will die of a disease in his blood.

(I am speaking Spanish so she does not understand.)

I tell her about Ramon, my alter ego, and about the sister who waits in vain.

I try to explain that I am in love with the one who cannot touch me because she does not know me except as the unnamed friend of her brother who, they say, dies in a prison riot.

Fragments of coloured glass cling to the soles of my feet like blood and ink. Every step I take leaves a trace that seems to form itself into a word.

Outside, the sky beyond the Sangre de Cristo Mountains is the colour of dead skin. Already the roads are clogged with pilgrims marching toward sanctuaries hidden in the hills. Some go home with their wives in the evening, only to return the next morning to resume their holy journey. Others trudge guiltily through the night, dragging heavy, wooden crosses, sipping sparingly from water bottles, denying themselves food and love and warmth.

At Pojoaque, the Christians take the right turn toward Chimayo.

Westward, the lights of San Ildefonso sparkle beneath the dark shape of Black Mesa, the Pueblo sacred mountain.

Climbing the cliff-face, Ramon discovers ancient pictographs drawn and abandoned over the course of centuries by anonymous Indian artists: herds of sacred animals, hunting scenes, spirals and winged snakes, humans disguised in skins and antlers, male and female genitalia.

It is a kind of code Ramon finds impossible to break, a mathematical equation he cannot solve. Yet his fingers trace the outlines longingly, as though they represent the walls of some protective haven.

A haven he cannot enter because inside they'll kill him.

From a distance he looks tiny and glows like a salamander.

I start to shiver.

You're cold, says Esmé. Her voice suddenly sounds exactly the way I would expect Ramon's sister's voice to sound.

Gently, she unties the enema bags and lifts the shower curtain from my neck. Naked, I see that I am turning blue from the cold. My body is wracked with chills that move over it like squalls across a lake.

What's going to become of you? she asks.

I don't know, I say. I will be ordinary too, and only dream of love and miracles. I cannot escape the story, I say, though every time I tell it I shall try.

She leads me into the bedroom and tucks me up against her breasts beneath the covers. We sip whisky from a bottle. In other parts of the house, her roomies are waking up.

Ramon quits the ledge of heiroglyphs and begins to scale the bare heights of the mesa. The only thing that feels good and safe is to keep moving, to keep climbing.

Restless, I disengage myself from Esmé's embrace. I find my clothes and start to dress. She crosses her arms over her breasts and frowns. Her hands are shrouded in long, black gloves. It's dreadfully cold. I wince as I pull my shoes on.

She catches my eye.

Her nipples are black and erect like nailheads. She has tiny, androgynous breasts. Her ribs press outward against her skin like the bars of a cage.

Doña Sebastiana.

She has become, or always was, that which I desire and fear most (also the woman to whom, years later, I say these words).

Her eyes glow with anger as I slip through the door.

Outside, the pilgrims are thronging the roads.

I step up beside a man whose knees are buckling under the weight of a redwood cross. The bark has been peeled away, and the wet wood shines like blood.


## The Dream of Life

This was a sort of daydream, which is to say, the mind dancing. The meaning of a story is only another story. The past is the meaning of the future. The future is the meaning of the past. The end is the sense of the beginning. But what is love, and what is the meaning of meaning?

Esmé was the one with her feet on the ground.

Recalling the pathetic note pinned to the sacristy wall, she filled the car with fried chicken, sodas and coffee, and together we drove to the prison (Jerusalem) where friends, lovers and relatives waited (like pilgrims) before the gate. They were mostly poor people, Indians, blacks and Chicanos. (We have ordained that the poor and the speechless will commit our crimes for us. All unknowing, torn by fear and anger, they make the sacrifice.)

In their sad eyes, I could see the wounds.

There was no one I would have taken for Ramon's sister. Nevertheless, I found a certain peace there, as Esmé knew I would, among the sinners. We understood that we had stumbled onto a holy place, a nexus where the plane of agony (Eternity) cut the plane of signs (Time).

Ramon had not escaped.

No one escaped.

That day or the next the prison authorities announced that all the inmates (dead ones, live ones and the ones with their heads cut off and stuck between their legs) had been accounted for. For them, at least, the riot had a satisfying statistical resolution.

The New Jerusalem remained inviolate upon the plain below the town.

Smoke rose from the ruined cell blocks. Sometimes, when the wind changed, a light, white ash would fall upon our heads like a blessing.

A black preacher began to speak. In his sad eyes, I could read the wounds.

We sang a hymn, and the dead were everywhere.

With the smoke rising and wet snow falling around us, we knelt in the mud and began to say the only words that could ever mean anything.

> Father, I stretch out my hand to Thee.
> No other help I know.
> If Thou withdraw Thy help from me,
> O Lord, whither shall I go?

But when I stand up, I am not changed and in my heart I am raging again. I am full of desire and hate. I want to throw myself away. I want to be the worst kind of son, so that when God finally takes my hand, it will prove that He really does love me. I want His forgiveness, His love, to be a test, not a reward. To me, that is the true meaning of the word *Father*, that I belong to Him, that He cannot abandon me, that He cannot cease to cherish me even though I cause Him the worst pain. Undeserved love is the only love I want. It's a horrible contradiction, I know. My impulses are all chaotic and self-destructive. I throw myself into the abyss, shouting, "Save me! Save me!" The terrible images of the prison riot only serve to excite and inspire me. They are a clue, a sign that something real has happened here. Emotional fallout is as tell-tale as the clicking of Geiger counters over ancient atomic bomb sites (Trinity). What I mean to say is only this: at the moment of slaughter, the killers (Ramon) were most open to themselves. This is often what it takes for a man to know the world. And when you ask yourself unanswerable questions, you come back to the beginning, like the man with his penis in his mouth. The truth is our bodies (lives, histories) are our metaphors, and the worm gnaws us all.

# WOMAN GORED BY BISON LIVES

1

Days, while my husband is at work, Susan and I make love on the couch in her parents' basement. It is a desperate thing to do, and we are both a little stunned by it. But something has pushed us to the edge of caring.

Gabriela, the baby, is upstairs sleeping, while Susan's mother does housework or watches soap operas. We keep our clothes on, manacled at the ankles by a tangle of underwear, jeans and belts. And when Susan comes, I press my palm across her lips to keep her from shouting out her joy.

I don't know if we are in love. But we are both in need of solace, and our sex is a composition of melancholy and violence, as though we are seeking to escape and punish ourselves in the same act.

The walls are decorated with hangings Susan made during a university art class. The weaving is sinuous and convoluted, with objects embedded or hidden in the loosely spun wool. They are analogues of a spirit which remains secret from me even at the height of passion. Her loom stands idle at the end of the room.

After sex, we lie together on the couch, our tops rucked up so that our breasts crush together, hot and soft, smoking dope and holding slides of Susan's work to the light. I profess to see themes, leitmotifs and images, and it is true that her work excites me with a mixture of admiration and anxiety (what is hidden; what is lost). But my insights are all superficial, and I cannot connect the woven mysteries with the woman who whispers or the woman who is Gabriela's mother.


Except during sex or when she is crying, Susan's face is expressionless. This is one source of my fascination with her. My own face is endlessly mobile and gives everything away. But Susan is always reserved, watchful and hidden. At first I took this for a sign of maturity and intelligence. She is tall and graceful, and her silence gives her the appearance of inner poise. I say *appearance*, because it is all a mask. Not even a mask, for the word *mask* implies that it is something she can put on or take off.

Susan's face is forever sad, and her sadness is her strength. Sadness has schooled her in waiting. Her expressionless face conceals her naïveté, her confusion, her lack. She is stunned — that's what her face means. She meets what she cannot understand with a blank stare and a few graceful gestures.


A photograph of Susan pregnant — suddenly, I see the significance of the objects hidden in the wall hangings. When I say it, she becomes angry.


Gabriela's father abandoned them before the baby was born. He is a violinist from Toronto. They met when he came to play in the city symphony. How they fell in love, how she became pregnant, seems now unclear in Susan's mind. What is clear is the way they finished. She has told me the story over and over. It is her national epic. It is how her life became the way it is: the baby, her return to Saskatoon and her parents' basement, the idle loom, her job in the composing room at the local newspaper.

The violinist wanted to marry her, she tells me. But his mother interfered. The three of them met — Susan pregnant, expressionless, watchful; the violinist cracking the knuckles of his sinewy, red hands; his mother fierce and excessively thin, calling Susan "my dear girl." The mother said he must not become entangled (like an object in one of Susan's pieces) so early in life or his career would suffer and he would end up mediocre (as she had done). "What she really meant," says Susan, "was that she could not bear to lose him, that he should take a different way." Now he is first violin in another town, his career is mediocre, and he writes wistful letters to Susan and his daughter.

Susan has learned to suffer in silence because there is nothing to say. The violinist and his mother took her voice, and she only dreams of saving enough money to move with Gabriela to a cabin at Pelican Narrows in the north. We make love quietly, secretly, in the long summer afternoons, while the baby sleeps and my husband works at his job at the oil company.

Susan has slept with one other woman. This was in Vancouver in her student days. The woman was her best friend, and they did it once, after a session posing nude for a photography class. "For lust," she says. "In the morning, when we woke up, I couldn't wait to get her out of my bed, out of my house. Do you understand?"

I have red, curly hair which I wear wild. I dress in faded blue jeans and hiking boots and a worn-out bomber jacket which used to belong to Danny, my husband. I wear three rings in my left ear and a butterfly tattoo above my pubic hair. Susan and I met during Louis Riel Day, when I rode a friend's quarter horse in the annual relay race and came second. She had Gabriela in a backpack and a bandana tied round her head. Her wire-rimmed glasses mirrored the crowds, the dust, the slick wet canoeists and sweating runners.

We walked along the riverbank together, away from the people (Danny was cooking steaks and burgers for some men's club he belongs to), Susan, quiet, indolent and graceful (later she confessed her nervousness, how she was so afraid of not making a good impression), and me, hot from the sun and the race. We crossed the railway bridge to the university side and hid among the trees. Susan put the baby down to play and undid her shirt to let the sun touch her breasts. When I kissed her, her eyes widened, her breath quickened. She took my hand and laid it between her breasts.


Danny is a sad man. He knows what's going on — up to a point. He knows I'm bored because he's bored. He doesn't like himself, so he's not surprised that I don't care much either. He plays ball in the summer, hockey in the winter. He's joined the Lions because his father was a Lion. Once a month he drives to the family place in the Qu'Appelle Valley for the weekend to check on his mother and talk to the neighbour who rents her last half-section of land. The old house needs paint and the barn is beginning to collapse.

He loves the place, but he could never earn enough money farming to make a go of it. He doesn't even like farming. He's got a good job publishing an in-house magazine for an oil company, but he's not a company man and hates the work. He dreams of selling up and moving to a cabin in the mountains to write a novel. But every novel he starts is about himself and he gets bored with it after the first four or five paragraphs.

He married me because I was different from the farm girls he knew growing up, those earnest, practical girls in jeans and white blouses. I almost laugh when I think of how he stared and stared at my tattoo. It's amazing what a tattoo will do to counteract the effect of a plain face and red hair. He thought I'd be the spark his novel was missing, the novel of his life. I married him for his bomber jacket. In this way we fall in love with things rather than people. It's only after you're married that you discover the recalcitrant baggage of personality attached to the bright, attractive object.

"We're at our best," says Susan, "when we have nothing to lose."

One day we take Gabriela and a picnic and drive north toward Prince Albert. We drink wine from a bottle along the way. The sun glares off the windshield, the wine bottle and Susan's glasses. She gives Gabriela a sip of wine and removes the little girl's shirt in the back seat.

We drive to Batoche and visit the battle site, then head for a nearby park and hike into the woods. It's a weekday so there is no one around. We take off our clothes and the baby's clothes. We lie together on a blanket with the food and wine around us, the hot sun warming the three of us, the naked baby crawling over our hot bodies.

Susan's cheeks are flushed. When I touch her, she shivers. For a while, we lie together, Susan with her back to me, my hand caressing her hair, her breasts, her sloping belly. Gabriela plays in the leaves. Later I take pictures of the mother and daughter together, then Susan pushes me down on the blanket and kneels between my legs and kisses me.

We get dressed as the afternoon wears on and drive further to an animal park where there are bison. Susan wants to see them; I want a photograph. There is a herd of cows and calves and one lone bull with a matted hump, but they are too far away for a decent shot. Gabriela and Susan walk a few steps, hand in hand, along the fence, pausing to pull up grass and hold it between the wires. I focus and focus, but nothing satisfies me. I am hot, light-headed from the wine and sun, anxious because all I can think of is the three naked females like goddesses under the hot sun.

It is difficult to describe precise states of mind. My style of abandonment is sentimental and hopeless. Sex is only a variant of nostalgia. I am so unhappy with Danny. I feel a quiver between my legs; I want something from Susan, something no one can give, want only perhaps that the afternoon will go on and on.

All at once Susan turns back to me and points the way we have come. A woman with a tiny Instamatic camera in her hand has crawled clumsily over the fence and is walking across the short grass toward the grazing cows. Her husband and two children stand outside the fence watching. I am looking through the viewfinder; Susan whispers something. I swing and sight the bull. He, too, is watching the woman with the Instamatic. His hooves drag at the earth. Shreds of old wool dangle in dusty hanks from his shoulder hump, like Susan's wall hangings.

I focus on the woman again, asking myself what dream has led her onto the buffalo prairie. A few moments before, we passed the couple with their children and heard her speak sharp words in a British accent. She is wearing a denim skirt wrapped around her bulging hips, a hooded sweatshirt, pink running shoes and thick glasses. Her lank hair flaps at her sunburned cheeks like crow wings. Her husband points, drawing the children's attention to their fearless mother.

I begin to shoot film as the bull dips his huge, awkward head and snorts. He trots in the woman's direction. She turns awkwardly and begins to run toward the fence, emitting high-pitched yips of panic, her Instamatic flapping on its wrist-strap. At the moment the bull reaches her, I stop winding the film forward; I shoot and shoot, exposing the same frame over and over.

### 2

Susan dies. This happens a year after we watch the bison gore the English tourist north of Batoche. She probably had the cancer even then, or so the doctor said. Danny leaves me sometime during that year, I forget when, though he still comes around to sit and visit. He does just sit, saying nothing. He still has nothing to say. But he has this impulse to comfort me with his company. He goes away angry because I can't be comforted, because I am outrageously inconsolable, because I have lost everything, because I just sit there smoking dope, sucking peppermint candies and crying in a room where the walls are covered with Susan's artwork.

The last one, the piece she did between the time we watched the bison gore the woman and the time Susan died hangs above my pillow. It's a bag woven of binder twine, frayed burlap and burst milkweed pods with their parachute seeds trailing down. Mornings I wake with milkweed seeds on my eyelids — usually I have dreamed Susan is kissing me. You can see the contents of the bag through the loose weaving: one of Gabriela's baby shoes, a dried up butterfly, photos of Susan and the baby naked, a plastic laminated newspaper headline. The bag was empty when she finished it; I am the one who placed these relics inside.


I develop the photographs from the afternoon at the bison park. I do this the same evening. Susan is as anxious as I am to see once again what we have seen: that lumpish, stupid woman, with her crow-wing hair, trotting toward the buffalo herd. Clearly, what we see in her is what we fear most in ourselves — ugliness and exposure.

But the pictures are a disappointment. The woman is too far away; the pictures are all sky and scrub prairie like the prairie snapshots amateurs take. The frame of multiple exposures shows only a tangled blur of movement, tiny bison legs, like fragments of prehistoric cave paintings, and an arc of white which could be the woman's face or her thighs.

The newspaper the next day tells the story: WOMAN GORED BY BISON LIVES. They are an immigrant family, freshly arrived from Saffron Walden. He is a fireman; she, a housewife. They had never seen bison before, had no idea they weren't as tame as cattle. Climbing that fence, the woman had simply wanted to get a better shot to send to her parents.

The bison's horn had severed an artery in her thigh, a potentially fatal wound — we had seen this and the aftermath: wardens shouting and flagging their arms to shoo the animals away, a man's hand pressed roughly against the wound, the tourniquet band twisted deep into her floury flesh, the husband's pale face as he held both children and looked about in shock.

Susan cuts out the article to keep.

We go to the hospital to visit the woman the bison gored. Her name is Ruth Hawking. We bring her flowers, chocolates (she looks like she eats a lot of chocolate) and magazines (magazines with photographs of thin, glamorous models). We go waltzing in with our gifts and shoo her surprised husband out the door. We say we read about the accident in the paper and thought we would like to cheer her up. Susan has made a special get-well card out of the photographs I took, gluing them together, end to end, in sequence, so that they unfold in an accordion panorama. When the woman sees the photographs, she starts to weep. The message on the card reads: WHAT IS WRONG WITH THIS PICTURE?

This is a cruel thing to do, but we have temporarily lost perspective. Actually, we are in the hospital for Susan's tests. Gabriela is with her grandmother; Danny is at the oil company. Susan and I are stoned. Her glasses keep falling down her nose. Last night I made her swallow five pearls so that the internist would have something good to look at when the X-rays were developed. "One thing," she says, "if this is bad, don't ever let me get un-stoned."

It's bad. Suddenly, all breasts become ominous objects, growths hanging clamped to your chest like limpet mines, getting ready to kill you. Only three pearls come out. We get the X-rays and look for the other two, holding the plastic negatives up to the light in Susan's basement. I'm shocked to see the white ghost bones and the fibre nets of Susan's organs.

She's still healthy, still makes love (later, her breath turns sour, and lumps appear like black pearls beneath her skin), only our love is more violent and perverse. She craves a pain she can enjoy. Her eyes are greedy for it. Perhaps it is some kind of voodoo she makes against the pain that will come later. Or (I never tell her this) perhaps it is only that she hates herself, that she sees herself as already dead, and only the pain can make her feel alive.

She throws her head back, her eyelids slip shut and she sighs, "Kill me, kill me" meaning "Save me, save me" or "Love me, love me."


Susan's real self begins to emerge. At first, as she loses weight, she is more beautiful than I could have imagined. The mask does not drop away, but it becomes more expressive, more complex in its implications (what it hides). She begins to weave again. She sits for hours at her loom with the baby on the bench next to her. She doesn't do this for the sake of art; it's so that Gabriela will retain an image of an industrious, capable mother. Gabriela, of course, has very little to say, but shows a surprising aptitude for entangling herself in whatever Susan is doing.

My obsession with photographing her (during this period, I take hundreds of pictures) seems morbid to Susan, but she puts up with it. I take photographs of all her activities: pictures of Susan cleaning house, sitting on the toilet, shopping, weaving, caring for Gabriela. I do a whole series of photos of Susan sleeping and another of Susan's face during orgasm. I do black-and-white studies of different parts of her body: hands, ear-lobes, nape of neck, nipples.

One day I follow her to work and spend an hour shooting her as she cuts the galleys into columns of print, waxes the paper and pastes the stories, headlines and ads onto her layout board. In her hands, the lines of type seem to curve and intersect like the cloth strands of her tapestries.

Secretly, we both know I am making provision for a future she will not share, getting ready for the time when she will be absent. She, too, is getting ready.

Nights, now that her parents understand our situation, I
sometimes sleep in her bed. (Nothing was said, only things
became, for them, suddenly clear; they have begun to treat
me with a certain gentle deference and formality which are
tokens of their affection.) In the middle of the night, I'll
wake up and watch her breathe. When she stirs, she sees
that I am weeping. "I miss you already," I say. "It hurts so
much I can hardly stand it." "What's the worst thing?" she
asks. "I'm afraid that when you die it will be awful, that
you'll choke or vomit and be terrified." She stares at me,
saying nothing, and I know I have said the words she would
have said herself.

We discuss Gabriela endlessly. Her parents are too elderly
to cope alone, Susan thinks. I say I want the baby, that I'll
take care of her because of the part of Susan that's in her.
Susan says, "Yes." But the next thing I know, she has made
up a questionnaire and mailed it to all her relatives and
friends. It begins, "I am dying of cancer. Soon my baby will
need a new family. You can help me decide what to do
about this by filling out and returning the following information sheet."

The things Susan wants to know include: "Do you believe life is a journey or a trial? Am I being punished?
What are your thoughts on hope? Has my life been a
waste? Will you continue to love and cherish my baby girl
even if she is a flop? How many times a day do you feel joy?
Have orgasms? What is the reason for men?"

After the forms come back, we make trips to conduct
interviews, until Susan finally decides to leave Gabriela
with an older sister in Medicine Hat. The sister has twin
boys a year old than Gabriela; her husband is an ex-rodeo
rider who owns his own air-freight business which special-
izes in transporting horses. "I want her to have some men

around," says Susan, "the kind of men that'll make up for her father." "What about me?" I ask. "You're her auntie. You'll always be there. You'll keep her from growing up ordinary. When the time comes, you'll tell her everything about me. She'll need to know."


One day (it's winter now) Danny and I take Susan and the baby to the city zoo. Danny is already looking for an apartment; our house is up for sale. Susan insists on carrying Gabriela as we walk among the pens and cages, until she gets tired and hands the baby to my husband. She leans on me as we walk; she's forgotten her mitts, so I give her one of mine, and we walk with our arms around each other, our bare hands buried in one another's coat pocket. To our surprise, Danny's good with Gabriela. He makes her laugh, holds her up to the fences to pet the animals and talks, talks, talks to her, though she never says a word back. "She's in love," says Susan. "She can't take her eyes off him."

We are all sad, feeling that, though we are together, we shall soon be apart for good. No one is angry. The level of disaster that has befallen us makes it seem impossible that any one person could have caused it. Walking through the zoo, we feel the dignity of companions in tragedy. We are not defeated, even though certain things are almost over, almost behind us. There is a sense in which I find this deeply satisfying. This is the way all life should be, I think, wishing only that Susan could go on dying, that my husband could go on leaving me, that we could forever be dispensed from living our humdrum lives — that desert of emotion.

We pause to smoke a joint at the bison pen, where the huge, lumbering beasts stand with their faces to the wind, chewing their hay. Susan and I are reminded of the day we watched the bull gore the woman from Saffron Walden. We have avidly followed Ruth Hawking's subsequent career in the papers — she has been arrested once for shoplifting and twice for reckless driving leading to minor accidents. Susan, always so restrained, gets the giggles whenever she sees these announcements. She says, "That woman the bison gored is *still* alive!"

The zoo bison look ungainly and alien, which they are, left over, as it were, from another time. The fences, the baled hay, the feeding rick and the low zoo buildings in the background, all contribute to this sense of dislocation. Except when seen attacking women, they are somewhat boring. They produce in me, for example, only a mild anxiety, a feeling that things aren't right, that there is much to be guilty for.

I look at Danny and say to Susan, "You know, he's not such a bad guy. I haven't been a very good wife to him." Susan starts to laugh. She gets hysterical and has to sit down on the cold ground. My hand is tangled in her coat pocket so that I fall down with her. Our laughter startles the bison, which glance warily in our direction.

Danny comes over with the baby to see what's wrong. Susan tells him what I said, that I haven't been a very good wife. Danny grins. He says, "That's an understatement." "That's what I said," says Susan, snorting with laughter. "Poor bunny," I say. "I'm sorry." He hands me the baby and helps us up. Tenderly, he pulls Susan's coat together at the throat and tucks her scarf in.


She watches. She soaks things up through her eyes. She stares at Gabriela for hours on end, hungrily absorbing every whim and turn of emotion. As she gets closer to the end, everything but the child becomes superfluous. "I don't want to forget her," she says. (What she means by this is a mystery about which I cannot bear to question her.)

About an hour before Susan dies, she opens her eyes and says to me, "Well, here we go." Her lungs begin to fill up, her breathing grows shallower. She makes a horrible bubbling sound in her chest, which I suppose is what they used to mean by the phrase "death rattle." Her mother holds her head. I sit on the bed, clutching Susan's hand.

Soon she is breathing air only into her throat. Then I think she must be dead, but her mouth keeps opening as though she were still breathing. It opens once or twice by reflex. I think this time she must really be dead. But then her chin moves once more and I feel a tremor in her hand. I say, "Go, baby sweetheart. It's okay. I'm here. You can go and not be afraid because we're here with you." Finally, she is dead, though I am not certain when the borderline was crossed, only that she is on the other side. Her mother lets her down and starts, through her tears, to sing a lullaby.

Susan's head is thrown back and slightly to the side, her mouth open. I recognize the pose. I've seen it in old paintings — it is the moment when the soul escapes through the mouth on its way to become a star. That's an out-dated mythological reference, I know, a leftover, like the bison. But I haven't got anything else. It just looks like that.

I go to see Ruth Hawking. (Her husband's name is in the new phone book.) This is a little pilgrimage for Susan. But Ruth is gone. She left him with the kids and flew back to Saffron Walden. Her husband, a lonely, harried man, tells me, "She had a difficult time adjusting to life in Canada."

He invites me in, but has nothing more to add, and I leave after a few awkward minutes. ("Men!" I say to myself.)


**3**


I go to Medicine Hat for a visit. I like the area. All of a sudden, it strikes me that I really want a place of my own just outside of town where the dry chinook winds blow endlessly in the caragana and nothing stops the eye. I take Gabriela for a drive to look at real estate. (I get a list from a broker.)

Communication is now possible, up to a point. We stop at a roadside table to eat our picnic lunch. I take out a ball of yarn and begin to teach her the Cat's Cradle. I don't really know how to make a Cat's Cradle myself, but I have brought a book and there is plenty of yarn. She is a reserved and intelligent child with Susan's eyes. Watching my fingers fumble with the yarn, her face becomes a mask.

I say to her, "There are certain things you have to know. Suicide is not an option. Life is always better under the influence of mild intoxicants. Masturbation is healthy, the sooner started the better. It's a sin not to take love where you find it. That is the only sin. I have photographs of your mother."